Sea Breeze

by

Lori Power

The Gentle Surf Series, Book One

This is a work of fiction. Names, characters, places, and incidents are either the product of the author's imagination or are used fictitiously, and any resemblance to actual persons living or dead, business establishments, events, or locales, is entirely coincidental.

Sea Breeze

Cover Art by *RJ Morris*

The Wild Rose Press, Inc.
PO Box 708
Adams Basin, NY 14410-0708
Visit us at www.thewildrosepress.com

Publishing History
First Vintage Rose Edition, 2017
Print ISBN 978-1-5092-1303-0
Digital ISBN 978-1-5092-1304-7

The Gentle Surf Series, Book One
Published in the United States of America

Arthur followed her

and then paused briefly on the threshold, pulled her tight against him, and kissed her brow. Then his heavy step echoed down the corridor.

She watched him depart. Elleah lingered, one foot in the hallway, hand on the door, and waited. He didn't look back. Once he had taken the turn to the stairwell, with a heavy heart, she turned back to her hotel room. Mid-stride, she stopped, surprise making her gasp.

Across the hall, another door stood open. Just inside the doorway, a tall man with heavy brows and a stern chin stared with open curiosity. Thick hair, bed tousled, made her wonder if he'd just woken up. His forearm braced against the jamb while he raised a glass with amber liquid to his mouth. Lips upturned in a casual smirk, he sipped. Over the crystal brim, his daring gaze coldly travelled the length of her flowered silk robe in frank appraisal.

Without confirming the robe had indeed fallen open to drape loosely across her breasts, Elleah turned on her heel and closed her door with a decisive click.

Praise for Lori Power

Dedication

To my mother—Joanne—who inspired this story
Happy Birthday!

Chapter One

Elleah spanned her hand across her brow to massage her temples. Breathing through her nose, she struggled to maintain her calm as she faced her brother's misguided indignation. In her quest for independence, she had chosen to use their mother's maiden name as her own.

"Jaundoo," Arthur barked and marched toward the hotel door. He paused, hand on the brass knob, turned, and trod back into the room to face her. "You're a Mellon, Elleah, and should be proud of it."

His temper reminded Elleah of when they were kids—arms overlapped across his barrel chest, nostrils flared. Red splotches colored his cheeks and her brother's yellow-flecked, deep green eyes burned with passionate indignation. His golden irises—like a sun shining through the branches in the forest—bored into her, willing her to bend to his command. But she would not bend. Not this time.

Some things never changed, and a part of her was glad. Placing her hands on her hips, not bothering to mince words, she leaned in closer to her older sibling. "Mama was a Jaundoo. I *am* proud of my name."

Arthur stood straight and dropped his arms. Hands fisted, he crossed the small suite, skirting the bed to pull the curtains aside and stare out the window to the expanse of golden beach beyond. The Mexican coastline was a shimmering mass, just visible on the horizon. The air heavy with heat and moisture, leaving everything the breeze touched with a tropical fragrance. Mid-morning sun blazed into the dim suite, casting a prism of color across the carpeted floor. His palm lay flat against the glass.

Did independence mean isolation? Elleah cursed the tightness of remorse rising in her chest, and tamped it down. She would be strong. But, frankly, she missed her family. The loss of her mother a little more than two years ago ached like an amputation.

To Elleah, who watched his rigid back, Arthur stood like a statue flawless—the ideal cosmopolitan man of 1950—tall, broad-shouldered, cultured, and precise. Picture perfect of a classic New Yorker. Groomed to be the man he'd become, he was fit and ready to take the reins of the Mellon family business.

She saw no future for herself in the banker's life.

Finally, he huffed and faced her. Pain stretched his features and caused his wide-set eyes to turn down. "Jaundoo's not *your* name. It's not the name *she* gave you."

Elleah, too, dropped her hands and changed tactics. Her affection for their proud heritage warred with her turmoil, the need for her own escape from the pain of loss. "What does the name Mellon mean to the likes of me? What did the mantle of Mellon ever do for Mother, God rest her soul, her whole life spent trying to fit in with a bunch of snobs who would never—will never—accept us for who we are?"

"Leave Mother out of this—"

"You brought her up," Elleah countered, legs braced and shoulders squared for argument.

Arthur's eyes misted slightly, and he bit his bottom lip. He raised his palms. "Father is a well-respected businessman. Our name means something in New York."

Her shoulders slumped. "Which is why I'm here. As far from New York as I can get." She swung toward the veranda, wrenching open the heavy patio door. "Now I'm Elleah Jaundoo, a jazz singer. Evening entertainment. No one knows me. No one expects anything from me. I don't have to be accepted, presented—or married, for that matter."

If her mother were still alive, Elleah would never have had to run away to escape her father's back room deal of foisting her off as just another contract. Her mother always stressed she had a choice.

Arthur's dark stare pinned her with its intensity. "You're everything to Father. You broke his heart when you left."

Elleah stepped out into the shade on the balcony. The fresh scents of the flowers below surrounded her, reminding her of grandmother's garden on the island of Trinidad. The tangy scent of the gardenias mixed with the earthy herbs and citrus, with an undercurrent of salt and seaweed. She pulled the weight of her hair off her neck and allowed the breeze to sweep away the heat. Pulling a large bloom to her nose, she sniffed. Like so much regret mounting within her, she recalled how long it had been since she'd been to the islands. "Don't tell him."

Arthur's face sagged, his mouth dropped and lost its light.

Her golden brother, the heir apparent, her childhood companion and confidant, looked much older than his twenty-eight years. Were those lines around his eyes new? She hadn't noticed them before, or the deep etchings to the sides of his full lips. Two years her senior, Elleah felt sorry for him. His normal cheerful appearance had deserted him. He'd tracked her all the way to California, only to be disappointed in his pursuit. His distinctive, squared features read like a novel to Elleah and stated quite clearly what he couldn't fix. For once, he couldn't make their father happy and make the situation right for the betterment of the family.

She stepped back into the room and faced her dressing table. She needed to be strong and hold back the tears that threatened. Bubbles of emotion churned in her stomach, and she was sick with despair. But this was the only way. Sighing with resolve, she crossed her arms over her chest.

Arthur's soft tread stopped behind her. His gentle hands rested on her shoulders.

Meeting his gaze in the mirror, she smiled. She noted how they shared the same narrow bridge of their nose and straight, uncompromising brow. Their eyes, too, were of a similar shape and color. However, two definite differences set them worlds apart. That he wore his features on a male body shrouded in creamy copper skin distinctly countered her café au lait complexion, proving the boundary of his acceptance and her isolation.

Her brother's countenance offered pride in family heritage: his elegant stance, trim figure, deep-set intelligent eyes, dark brows, and wavy black hair.

She, too, was blessed with a lot of her father's traits—emerald eyes, a determined and stubborn personality; however, she also carried her mother's petite, slender frame, throaty voice, and Caribbean heritage.

Since her mother's death a little over a year ago, Elleah endured a continuing quarrel with her father over marriage and her place in the community. Elleah was done with the pretense. "If I'm not accepted by them, Arthur, I won't accept them, either."

"You've not even given *them* a chance. Heaven's sake, you refused to be presented." He sighed. His fingers tightened on her shoulders. "Not even for the sake of our father?"

"To honor the memory of our mother." Elleah stepped away from his touch. "I will use the gifts she had me cultivate since I was a little girl. I will sing and play the piano, as she taught me. I will earn my living and establish my place through the talent she provided, not from the privilege afforded me."

Arthur turned her to face him and placed a thumb under her chin so she met his gaze. "He made her happy, you know. They were happy together…right to the end."

His gesture easily broke the walls she erected around her heart. Elleah took his hand and squeezed. "Yes, he loved her and she him, but the life killed her. The constant disappointment. The ever-present need to prove herself worthy."

Their mother never complained, but Elleah remember the painstaking care her mother took before each outing, every dinner party, business engagement and for what. When it came time to present Elleah into this "polite" society, her mother had to grovel for a place for her daughter. Right to the end, her mother seemed to beg for a position which should have been established and not have to be constantly earned.

"You're wrong, you know." He lowered his brow to touch hers. "You've created memories based on assumptions."

"Have I?"

"Gossip," Arthur countered.

"Like a knife, words wound, too."

Arthur lifted his head and nodded.

Was he done with the argument he realized he couldn't win?

"She was better than all of them." He pulled her into a hug and rested his cheek on the top of her head. "You're better than all of them."

Elleah melted into his familiar embrace, the fight dissipating. "Then leave, Arthur. Forget you found me. Make him understand I had to go. I need a life of my own where I am judged for who I am *really*. Not who I am because of a name. Not the badge of our father's business mistake."

Arthur jumped back and held her shoulders at arm's length. "Mother was never a mistake, don't say that. Not ever!"

Throat tight, Elleah hung her head, her hair swinging forward. "I know," she whispered. "I'm sorry."

Arthur shook her slightly. "Don't say that again. Not ever. Don't even think it."

She met his gaze and nodded. The lump of emotion clogged her breath and the words wouldn't form.

"He won't give you up," Arthur said, gripping her shoulders hard enough to bruise. "You're his daughter. He loves you. He won't walk away."

She wouldn't flinch. Inhaling deeply, she filled her lungs and again stepped back from his touch. Head high, she strode across the room, stopped at the heavy door and swung it open. Swallowing back the thickness in her esophagus, she locked gazes with her brother. "He has to. Forget about me. Leave me to live a life I carve out for myself. Independent. Free."

Arthur followed her and then paused briefly on the threshold, pulled her tight against him, and kissed her brow. Then his heavy step echoed down the corridor.

She watched him depart. Elleah lingered, one foot in the hallway, hand on the jam. He didn't look back. Once he had taken the turn to the stairwell, with a heavy heart, she turned back to her hotel room. Mid-stride, she stopped, surprise making her gasp.

Across the hall, another door stood open. Just inside the doorway, a tall man with heavy brows and a stern chin stared with open curiosity. Thick hair, bed-tousled, made her wonder if he'd just woken up. His forearm braced against the jamb while he raised a glass with amber liquid to his mouth. Lips upturned in a casual smirk, he sipped. Over the crystal brim, his daring gaze coldly travelled the length of her flowered silk robe in frank appraisal.

Without confirming the robe had indeed fallen open to drape loosely across her breasts, Elleah turned on her heel and closed the door with a decisive click.

Chapter Two

The breath of a husky musical note carried across the sea breeze and drew Reginald Cavanaugh back from the ocean's edge. His toes squelched in the soft sand. He reached a hand to sweep his hair out of his eyes and back under his fedora. The surf brushed against the rolled cuff of his casual trousers. He glanced one way, and then the other down the long stretch of Southern Californian beach before turning his attention back to the prominent Hotel Del Coronado.

Jazz? In the early afternoon? Only on Coronado, he thought with a wry twist to his lips.

The sun blazed like a God seeking accolades, and the beach sparkled with the golden shimmer of pyrite. The resort certainly had its own ambiance. But, he wasn't ready to go back to the hotel and family expectations, just yet. Would he ever be ready? He supposed he'd have to face the situation at some point. Not yet.

He bent to scoop up a pristine shell. Within the hard contours of the outer casing, soft blue and greens, mixed with a pale peach, were perfect. His sister would love such a treasure found randomly on the beach. Maribel always fancied gifts where no money had been attached. She often accused their parents of trying to buy their affection. Reginald smiled; if only they could understand, unlike him, Maribel could never be bought.

Reginald adored Maribel and her carefree ways. He tried to visit as often as he could. Unfortunately, the care facility where their parents had placed his sister restricted access, and given his schedule… He shook his head. That was no excuse. He knew he was trying to assuage his own guilt—but remorse filled him like an hourglass.

His ears perked. Again, the melody touched him like a tender caress. Concentrating, over the tenor of the surf, he made out some of the words. A familiar song streamed from the beach lounge's open patio doors. Turning from the gentle current, he made to walk back to the hotel.

"Reggie?" Catherine's hand on his forearm stalled his intended motion across the shimmering sand. "Where are you going?"

He glanced first at Catherine's manicured fingers before adjusting his gaze on her shaded face hidden under the brim of the over-large, blue-striped hat. Between the pull of the song and thoughts of his beloved sister, for a moment he forgot why he was there and why this tall willow of a woman stood at his side.

Unwilling to provide an answer, given he didn't quite understand why the melody pulled at him. Reginald shook his head and swiped at an invisible fly.

Then the weight of expectation spread its burden across his shoulders and he remembered. Catherine Burr and her family had expectations. The same hopes possessed by his own family. That was why the Burrs had joined the Cavanaugh clan at the seaside. This was the week his father, Declan, would put down his foot and demand Reginald become a man and take his rightful place at the bank. A proper banker, of course needed a wife. And let's not forget the political potential with the right name and placement. Within a few years, a marriage to the heiress Burr would further the family fortunes from the east to the west coast.

Well, it was the plan, of sorts—his as well. Secure his future—his fortune, and make a name for himself independent of his father's massive influence in their home state of New York. This was what he wanted, what he had worked the last years to achieve. So, why now was he experiencing so many doubts? Why, at the pinnacle moment, was he burdened with distractions?

He shook his head to clear the haze, get a grip on his thoughts, and concentrate on the goal so close at hand. "My God, look at 'er, Catherine." He tactfully stepped away from her cold, fish-like fingers and pointed back to the red-topped, iconic Hotel Del Coronado. "Here we are, midway through the century and yet the Del transports one back in time, so one could swear the year was still 1928, before the world changed forever."

One hand on her hat brim, she tilted her chin to look up at him. "Oh, Reggie, how you make me laugh." She tittered and stepped closer.

Her strong lavender scent assaulted his nose, working in contrast to the crisp sea air. Reginald recoiled internally from her nearness. His breakfast sloshed uncomfortably in his stomach.

Her brow furrowed and the lines between furrowed, making her look significantly older than her twenty-four years. She wouldn't age well.

"How would you know?" Catherine continued, waving a hand in to encompass their surroundings.

"You weren't even born."

He bent to unroll the trouser cuff and moved toward their beach chairs. Standing, he paused again. The smoky voice sailed over the wind and beckoned him forward. Reginald walked on to the hotel, leaving Catherine to follow at her leisure. He longed to forget about the woman at his side and his obligations. He snatched up a red-striped hotel towel off the chaise.

Why did he care who was singing? He had no great love of music. Enjoyment, yes, but he was not a connoisseur. Like most cultured men, groomed as he was to step into his father's shoes, he graduated from Stanford. Determined to create a well-rounded man, his parents had instilled an appreciation of the arts, but Reginald never went out of his way to attend the great concerts. The exception would be when there was a lovely woman to impress. Then sitting through the masters' series was certainly worth the tedium for the reward to follow.

Catherine reached her pale, long fingers along his sleeve to stall him again. "What's the hurry, Reggie? We're not expected for some time yet. Walk with me."

He studied her long, horsy face—too strong for a woman. Her wide-set feral eyes calculated his every move and monitored his behavior, tallying his deficiencies. Yet, like him, she was still willing to pursue the only stud worth the bet. Or, better put, the only one her parents would allow, given the social game.

He searched the horizon for an escape. The whole situation, which had sounded so perfect in the planning, now turned his stomach. How could he throw away his life on a woman who thought so little of herself? She was strong and reliable, and he admired her tenacity related to the causes she represented, but when she meekly bowed to the potential of marrying a man she knew had no great affection for her, he lost respect.

On more than one occasion, Reginald had been obliged to accompany Catherine to the opera. They meshed well socially. Their family connections saw them in the best circles. This boded well for his father's political aspirations. But, despite his previous schemes, Reginald had no real interest in a long future with Catherine. The fact that his father had brokered a deal with Catherine's father, Peter, and now demanded his acquiescence, smarted—and he felt obliged to rebel as though he were still a teenager.

Reginald coughed to distract her. "Excuse me, Catherine." He lifted her chilled fingertips to his lips. "I missed what you said. Perhaps I've had a bit more sun today than I realized. Let me escort you to your room to rest before lunch."

She nodded and tucked a stray lock of hair, caught in the growing gust, back under her hat, then she fitted her fingers smoothly in the crook of his arm. "Of course." Her open face couldn't hide her disappointment. "That would be nice."

He turned his cheek when she leaned in for a kiss. A life with Catherine Burr would have him evading her disappointed look over and over again, to the point where he would become a carbon copy of his father. Perhaps this realization came from spending so much time with her in preparation for launching a life together. Whatever the reason for his clarity, Reginald felt the walls push in around him and like a mouse evading the cat, he was looking for the exit.

Leaving his betrothed by her door, Reginald walked away considering how he would manage to avoid lunch. By the time he entered the lounge area, all that was left of the former occupant was a lingering scent of freshness. An earthy-citrus odor, which stood out next to sultry scent of leather and cigar smoke. Disappointed to find the place empty, he returned to his room. There, he paced from the veranda, to the bathroom, to the liquor cabinet and back again, haunted by the weight of expectation. So far, he'd downed two scotches and the little hand on the clock had hardly touched the three.

Disappointed and empty, he couldn't put a finger on what had triggered this change. He added ice to his glass. The chunks clinked in merry delight as he poured the amber liquid. The mugginess of the weather caused everything to puddle. The short-sleeved knit shirt, so fashionable on the east coast clung to him where the sweat ran down his spine. Until his arrival at the Del, he had been all for the matrimonial plan he and his father had conceived. What had altered?

Despite his foul mood, he couldn't get the melody of that damned song out of his head. He switched on the radio. Nat King Cole's "Mona Lisa" crooned through the speaker system and offered no respite. Mid-motion, hand on the dial to change the station, the sharp rap of knuckles against heavy oak echoed off the walls. Reginald's attention was drawn to the door.

Reginald prayed for a day when some ingenious inventor would come up with automatic locking doors. On this thought, his father knocked twice and entered.

"Have you closed the deal yet?" Declan began without preamble, helping himself to the contents in the liquor cabinet. "This…" His arm swept the general area. "What would you call it…courtship?…is all well and fine to those who can afford to take the time. But we have plans, my boy, and we need the Burr money to execute."

Contemplating the balcony as a possible escape route, Reginald pinched the bridge of his nose. Did he need to be reminded yet again about his "duty" to his family? His responsibility for the continuation of their prosperity? How, if they didn't continue to grow and expand, the Cavanaugh bank may as well give up and lose generations of hard work?

No.

And, yes.

Reginald slumped down on the chaise, then stood again, almost immediately to join his father at the cabinet. He topped up with scotch, forgiving the ice for melting. He downed the liquor in one gulp, neglecting to enjoy the smooth burn as it descended to his near-empty stomach. He set the crystal on the smooth wooden tabletop. "Marriage is not a 'deal.' This is my life. So, no, I have not yet asked Catherine to wed."

"Already implied."

"Not yet," Reginald countered. He should have held his tongue. The liquor dulled his defenses.

"By God, it's a contract, and dammit, boy, we've no time for this." His father's high color purpled around the edges. The sharp bones of his skull gave every illusion of a ghoul come to life. "It's expected." Declan rattled the ice in his glass. "Everyone knows the marriage will happen. Peter Burr and I have drawn up the paperwork for the future financing. You know the Burr money is essential to the growth of the Cavanaugh empire. We'll never take California without it. Catherine may as well put the ring on her own finger and pick out the drapes."

"Father…" Reginald huffed and reached for the bottle, noting its contents were almost drained. "I simply—"

"No." Declan slammed his heavy glass down with a clatter. "No. We haven't the time or inclination for romantic subtleties. No more discussion. We've come to terms. You're my heir. Act like it."

Chapter Three

Most of the tables were occupied in the lounge area shaped like a cloverleaf. The three alcoves featured more privacy seating for larger parties. At the front, the band vied for control over the room loud with boisterous conversation. The tall windows stood open to the early evening breeze and provided a breathtaking view of the sunset.

Reginald avoided the lure of salty-sweet snacks. Reaching instead for the decanter, he filled his glass, and leaned back in his chair. Leather cushions molded comfortably beneath his tall frame. He had joined Declan and Catherine's father, Peter, at a round oak table situated at the back of the smoky room, to enjoy the entertainment.

A pause between the first and second acts provided time to further discuss the plans for expansion. Declan, with the precision of a surgeon, steered the conversation always focusing on the future, avoiding the pitfalls of the present. Reginald took mental notes. Plan and push forward—always. Given the opportunity, he too would pull off such feats in future dealings with Peter to get to the end game. Control over the west coast and create a banking empire.

The band's drummer thrummed a quick beat interspersed with cymbals to announce the change in entertainment. At the raised dais, a glittery figure swayed to a new rhythm. She lifted the microphone to her mouth and her hum complemented the band. Reginald sat straighter in his chair. The first notes reached him and the hair on the back of his neck stood at attention. He sat forward and braced his elbows on his knees and peered at the pixie-like woman. Not only did he recognize the singer, hers was the voice that had drawn him from the water's edge earlier.

"That's a mighty big voice from that tiny little girl up there," his father drawled to Peter Burr, elongating an accent rarely heard in the boardroom in New York.

Reginald turned his head toward the older men and smiled indulgently. Captivated by the moment, in every note she sang, a rush of gooseflesh ran along his arms. With an unhurried air, he brushed his palm along his bare forearm and sat back in his seat. He resumed a casual posture, arm slung over the back of the chair, and a foot laid on his knee to enjoy the music. Interested in both the conversation at the table and the mysterious neighbor from across the hall, Reginald decided to bask in the atmosphere and after-dinner drinks. Fortunately, the ladies had retired for the evening, leaving the men to their cigars and scotch so he had no need to invent idle chitchat.

The thought of his mother and Catherine made Reginald cringe internally. Already, he felt his life had taken on a routine outside his control. When had he decided to travel this road? Was there ever a choice? Despair encircled him like the blue smoke from the cigarettes. He stared through the haze toward the raised stage, which stood to the side of the band.

The entertainer gave every impression of a life carefree. What kinds of expectations did she have? The songbook? She showed up and that was that. No complications, no hassles, no life altering decisions and no one to be tied to for the rest of her life. At that moment Reginald knew he would throw everything to the wind to feel that kind of freedom of choice and control over his own destiny.

He nodded at the two men and agreed with his father; the woman certainly had a big voice. But she also had so much more. Alone, with the lights illuminating her figure, she captured the imagination in ways a man promised to another woman should not be tempted. Her hair sat high on the crown of her head, giving her the impression of height he knew she lacked. Earrings danced with refracted light. Bejeweled and regal, she sparkled from head to toe. But she may as well have been unadorned as she offered her voice for presentation to the audience.

Scanning the crowd, comprised mostly of men, he couldn't help but wonder how many in the room wished they knew what he knew—her room number. A satisfied grin spread across his face and he reached a finger to stroke the stubble above his lip. Reginald relished the warmth of knowledge while he basked in the tempo of the velvet melody.

Fingers thrumming in place above his mouth, he pursed his lips contemplating the singer. How different she appeared this evening compared to his first glimpse of her shapely figure the day before. Her voice carried and the chords drew him like an ancient tug. As he watched her move, her curves accented by the red draped fabric, which rounded over her hips to fall in a puddle around her ankles, he pictured her as he had seen her yesterday—the neckline of her robe skimming the mounds of her breasts, nipples suggested through the thin silk—smooth skin, begging to be touched.

Or, so he imagined touching her. He was veering into his own imagination. Glancing around the area to the men present, their unwavering attention to her movements, he considered his fantasies were likely shared.

"Reginald," Declan barked. "Are you lost?"

Without altering his posture, Reginald swung his gaze toward his father. Used to the old man's behavior, especially after too many drinks, Reggie raised an eyebrow in question. "Perhaps," he said with a smile and a wink. "The music has me captivated."

"You and every man in here." Peter reached to slap a hand across Reginald's knee in agreement.

"Yes, well." Declan cleared his throat.

Reginald pulled his focus back to the older men, knowing from long experience what was coming.

"Back to the business at hand."

"If we must." Reggie returned and swung his long legs forward to face the men. Setting his glass on the side table, he rested his elbows on his knees.

His father gave him a hard glare. "Yes, we must."

Reginald concentrated on Peter. His slouched and saggy face provided the perfect disguise for a brilliant and cunning brain. Reginald trod carefully, leaving the conversation to flow as it would. Peter was a robust man with a big opinion and an even bigger ego. Easily offended, or so Declan had advised, many deals were lost due to people underestimating Peter's potential.

"Catherine's a good girl," Peter began, his double chin wobbling with expression. He scratched his nose. "She'll make a mighty fine wife."

Reginald reached for the glass, changed his mind, and linked his fingers together. Could he really chain himself to this kind of existence for the rest of his life? All for the sake of a few million dollars? Was his life not worth more?

"Granted her mother only gave me the one, no son, no spare, I can't guarantee she's a breeder." Peter coughed to cover the indelicate discussion before continuing. "Catherine's mother died at the end of the war. Bad timing," Peter suggested. "But I blame myself, really."

Many, in their social circles in New York, suggested suicide. Reginald met his father's stare and compressed his lips. Neither would offer condolences or comment unsure of how either would be received. On this, Reginald knew they were of one mind.

Declan seemed intent on keeping the conversation moving. The older man reached into the bowl and scooped out a handful of peanuts. Tossing a couple into his mouth, he crunched them loudly. "We must have heirs," Declan added, pointing to an imaginary piece of paper on the table. "We'll have to include a clause to cover that point in the agreement."

Though they discussed options, Reginald hadn't even consented, yet they proceeded with their plans as though he had. In supposition, his agreement was implied based on his lack of disagreement. What a tangled web to reach the ultimate goal. Would it be possible to include Peter without the implied marriage to his daughter?

Unlikely.

The two men had moved past the formalities and were now discussing the finer points of their expected expansion into the West once the merger was complete.

"Los Angeles is still full of gunslingers and starlets," Declan muttered, leaning back in his chair and wiping beads of sweat from his prominent brow. His hair had long since receded, leaving him with a pale dome and a comb-over. He turned his attention to the music and puffed his cigar. "Everyone here is waiting for their big break."

Peter's gaze joined Declan's and Reginald watched as the duo focused on the singer. A mammoth of a man, Peter had eyes like a lion. His future father-in-law wore an expression of hunger—eyes eager, lips slightly parted, and moist. Reginald imagined a drop of drool forming at any moment. He could read the man's appetite for the petite entertainer and wondered if his soon-to-be relative had already bargained for her after the show. Was she for sale? The thought of the lovely lady with the likes of this hulking man turned his stomach and a flare of jealousy flamed his skin. While imagining her in his bed whet his appetite, the image of her with likes Peter gave him the urge to punch the obese man in the jaw just for thinking of the singer that way.

The Del booked talent significantly more upper class than the New York entertainers Reginald was used to. By the look of her outfit alone, he surmised she didn't moonlight in the seedier locations—yet had he not seen a man leaving her room the morning before?

His table company had fallen quiet again and Reginald followed the men's attention back to the stage. Watching her, hearing the words, made it easy to drift with her song. The melody draped over him. Her voice enveloped him in a suggestion of warmth and comfort he'd yet to experience in his own life.

Her eyes were closed and her hips swung in time with the orchestra. Both hands caressed the microphone, and she sang into the amplifier as though she were making love.

Reginald felt an arousal picturing himself making love to such a woman. The sun fully set, the image of the two of them on the beach formed in his mind. He reached for the decanter and filled his glass, then passed it over to his father, to distract his own wayward thoughts.

Declan lifted a finger off the crystal and pointed toward the crowd. Well dressed and moneyed, the customers of the Del gave every impression of wealth. "Theirs is the money we want," Declan declared. The decanter banged against the tabletop, shattering the moment. "They have lots of it."

Reginald sipped his drink and surveyed the men from under drooped lids. He couldn't blame them for their planning—scheming. Hell, he had planned for this, too. Owning the largest chain of banks in the US was an easy allure. He dreamed of single ownership—his banks stretching from one coast to the other. No partners, no board, no one to tell him how to run his affairs, and Catherine, he sighed internally, deflated just thinking of the willowy blonde. She was though, simply a means to an end. He had led his father and Peter to these expectations. He had sown the seeds, with Catherine as well. So, what was holding him back now? He stood abruptly.

Peter started at the sudden movement and sloshed his drink over the rim. Driblets ran down the sides of the glass and dropped on his trousers. "My God, man."

He transferred the glass to his other hand and flapped his fingers, freeing them of the moisture. "What's the matter?"

Reginald took the handkerchief from his pocket and offered it to Peter. "One too many drinks, I think," he lied. "Perhaps I need a bit of air, to sober up if I'm to keep up with you two?" He offered a smile to compensate.

Peter accepted the folded material and brushed stray droplets from his pants leg. "If you're gonna play with the big boys, Reggie, son, you'll have to learn to hold your liquor." The large man paused to swing his attention to Reginald's father. "Am I right or am I right there, Dec?"

Declan's bushy brows drew down across his nose before his face cleared.

His father wasn't fooled, and his narrowed look told Reginald he knew just how much, in the line of spirits, Reginald could hold. Reginald ignored the unasked question, nodded, and said, "We'll be sailing tomorrow…early."

****

Elleah stood in her room, by the patio doors, contemplating the bed or balcony. The breeze fluffed the gauzy curtains away from the window. Elleah watched the lights from the lampposts flicker across the sand. She crossed the threshold out onto the veranda. Who was she fooling, she couldn't sleep. Occupational by-product of singing until two a.m. The hotel was quiet, and she needed time to wind down. Standing in a room of hungry wolves for hours made her cautious.

Her nose flared with the sweet scent of garden flowers and salty air. The combination calmed her.

Contrary to her bravado with her brother, Arthur, her profession in this new life had several drawbacks, not least of which was fending off men's curiosity and wandering hands. Some women stayed the whole show, but many held to old traditions and typically left after the first break. Would these traditions of wives leaving their husbands after supper to their drinks and baser entertainment ever end? Shouldn't the married woman be equal to an evening out instead of being relegated back to the children?

Elleah sighed. These were no longer her concerns. She had fled from that life of expectation.

She threaded her fingers through her hair and loosened the strands from their tight confines. As the tresses flowed over her shoulders, she gently braided them into a loose tail. Sure, she loved the stage— performing the songs, expressing herself for who she was, and feeling the moment; however, when she stepped down off the dais, life became a little more interesting than what she had been brought up to expect of men.

She shivered and huffed, and then threw the braid back over her shoulder. Until the last months, men in her presence treated her with gentlemanly grace and manners. Difference that was her due based on breeding and societal expectations. Comparatively, these men who watched her entertain them here at the Del, with her songs had the groping hands of an octopus. The aftermath of stage life made her feel dirty. Their lewd suggestions would have brought both her father and brother to fisticuffs in her defense. But she had learned, in a very short period of time, to smile and disengage without offense. Was the freedom really worth the risk?

She pulled the bobs from her ears and unclasped the chain from around her neck. The set had belonged to her grandmother. Many would assume them costume jewelry. She had no intention of alerting them to the contrary. Making up her mind, Elleah stepped back into the room and walked toward her dressing table. She dropped the jewels in the box, and stashed it in a drawer. Dropped her robe on the side of the bed, she stepped into a lightweight dress. She adjusted the straps across her shoulders. Pausing on the threshold, she returned to the closet to retrieve a sweater.

The music of the ocean breathing in and out on its tidal flow, combined with the salty air that both refreshed and relaxed her as she strolled along the boardwalk. The people sounds were slight and she could imagine she was alone in the world. Slipping off her sandals, she stepped onto the sand, her feet sinking into the moist coolness. The roll of the current beckoned. The farther she wandered down the beach, the more the night embraced her. High clouds scuttled across the sliver of a moon, and the stars grew brighter.

The sea danced to and fro. The water edged in to tickle her feet, only to race back out to the ocean's depths, in the constant catch-me-if-you-can momentum of each small wave. Elleah smiled at her nonsensical thoughts and wished her mother were with her to share the moment. Her mother, Josiah—Josie for short, had been a woman captivated with imagination. She could make stories out of the clouds, envision faces in the mountain ranges, hear the songs sung in the whisper of the wind rustling the leaves, and see the dance of those trees swaying to the music of the breeze.

Elleah swiped a tear off her cheek and turned from

her trance to wander farther down the beach. She had walked only a short way, skipping over the incoming surf, when she landed wrong, tripped, and fell over—legs.

Chapter Four

A sharp pain jolted Reginald awake. Followed closely by a high-pitched cry, he shot to his feet, only to bend and grab at his own bruised shin and fall back onto the sand. He landed heavy on his backside, grabbing for his lower leg. He blinked several times trying to get a grip on the chaos that suddenly surrounded him. Lulled by the music of the surf and the serenity of being by himself, he had fallen asleep on the beach. This was not how he had anticipated waking.

"What's going on here?" he bellowed, searching the dark for his tormentor. He bent forward to massage his aggrieved limb. Aside from a circling gull, no one answered.

Skimming his fingers along the bone, he could detect lingering soreness. Reassured his leg was undamaged, he stood and peered around. Over the sounds of the ocean, he heard a sigh and gasp off to his right. As though it would assist with his sight, he lifted a hand to his brow, squinted his eyes, and peered into the darkness. He couldn't see clearly, the night offered only shadows for companions. "Who's there?"

Finally, after a pregnant pause, a woman spoke. "Who are *you,* and what are *you* doing on the beach?"

Her aristocratic voice whipped out at him on the breeze, but within the depths of her throaty tones held a note of a tremor. He was sure she held back tears. The last thing he needed just now was a hysterical female. Reginald had come to the beach specifically to avoid such drama. He adjusted his weight from one foot to the other, burying his feet in the sand in the process. The bruise on his shin was hardly a lasting injury. Bred to be a gentleman, he leaned toward the sound of her voice and softened his tones. "Are you hurt?"

The silhouette moved and then slumped. A groan, followed by a soft *umm*, offered the answer. "No," she squeaked.

He chuckled. Perhaps the woman thought he was drunk or posed some other threat. Certainly a possibility and he couldn't fault her for thinking cautiously. Carefully, Reginald knelt on the sand, close enough to make out a fragment of shape, the white of eyes catching the smallest amount of light illuminating minor details of the slight form. The fact that she was curled, hunched over her knees with one drawn up to her chest and the other stretched in front, confirmed his suspicions of injury.

Taking one step, he reached out a tentative arm. "Here, let me see," Reginald said in a voice reserved for his horse, Sadie.

"I'll be fine." She inched a little away on the sand.

The tang of her voice was haughty—Boston? Maybe. The quality was both foreign and familiar. "I doubt you are a physician."

He smiled at her astuteness. "I may not be a physician, but I can certainly tell a sprain from a break—"

"I'm fine on my own, thank you."

Intrigued, he wondered at her origins, positive she was not Californian. He stayed where he was and waited. Her accent defined her as being from the east coast, with a touch of an exotic inflection over some of the vowels. Though her tone offered a clear dismissal, he grinned, captivated by the moment. "I'd be some kind of cad if I left a lady stranded, possibly injured on the beach." He paused and considered her, wondering if she were married and what her husband would think of her down on the beach with a strange man. "And just what is a lady doing out here—alone—on a beach in the middle of the night?"

The shadow sat up straight. "And just what are *you* doing on the beach at this hour...sir?"

With the sound of her voice, he imagined eyes flashing with her whiplash words. She held the last vowel like an accusation. The darkened outline rounded up on her knees, struggled to her feet, teetered, and held her balance on one foot. Peering through the dark, he wanted to see more. She had him fascinated.

The flash of white teeth caught in the dim light.

Was she biting her lip? He'd like that. He pictured a full lip caught between lovely teeth, and his loins tightened. Reginald reached out and snagged her by the shoulders before she could fall over. The bones of her upper arms were slight, but muscles surrounding them seemed strong.

Her breath heaved on an outward rush of, "Oh."

He stepped closer, enjoying the tang of salty air mixed with flowers and expensive cigars. "Sleeping."

"Wh-what?"

He smiled, enjoying the off balance, the intrigue, and most of all, the blindness of the moment. For a long time, Reginald had followed the lead of others and lowered his expectations. Life had turned typical and it had been too long since he was interested. In this moment, he had to use all of his other senses, aside from visual, to form his impressions and this newness, created an intense curiosity.

The silhouette moved. She stood rigid and her head, held high, still barely reached his shoulder.

He heard the hiss of an indrawn breath. "Sleeping," he repeated. His thumb wrapped around her upper arm. He could only imagine the body sheathed under the silky dress. "You asked what I was doing on the beach. I was relaxing, enjoying the ebb and flow of the ocean, and must have drifted off. The next thing I knew, something, or should I say someone, jumped on me."

"I-I did not." She pulled back from his touch. "I certainly did not *jump* on you. I didn't see you."

Unwilling to release his hold, he stepped closer. "I'll walk you back to the hotel." Reginald moved his grip to her elbow. "I'm assuming your husband will be missing you."

"I don't—there isn't," she gasped, paused, and then drew in a deep breath. "I am fine on my own. Thank you for your assistance."

With a steadying hand, Reginald retained his hold, but replaced his grip with his left hand and moved his right to the small of her back. He was inordinately pleased at her discomfiture and her unmarried status. "Off you go, then, Miss..." He released her elbow and let the question hang—hoping.

"Miss—" She stopped, swiped his palm from her lower back. The petite form hobbled a step, teetered, and would have fallen had Reginald not acted quickly, grabbing her up in his arms. Her palms flattened against his chest, and at this close proximity, he recognized her.

He should have known from her throaty voice. He must have really passed out to be this dim witted. She was his neighbor. The woman who had captured his imagination both visually and aurally. A woman who stood scantily clad in her robe while a man left her quarters mid-morning. The lounge singer who held the notes a heartbeat longer than necessary, as though she were living with the music.

****

The distance back to the hotel wasn't far, but the duration to get across the sand seemed like it may take forever. With the uneven, unforgiving beach, Elleah thought she'd never make it on her own. She glanced across the expanse to where trim lights edged the boardwalk. What choice did she have? She was stuck dependent on this man. She wanted to cry with the frustration.

The pain in her ankle throbbed, keeping pace with her heartbeat. Did her rescuer have to be *him*? Elleah stared up at the familiar, rugged face from across the hotel hallway.

"Jaundoo." He answered his own question, and grinned in a cocky way.

Her heart thumped loudly before slamming against her ribs. The darkness fled as she took in his features. Now that she recognized him, all of his characteristics came into focus. The grin etched by his white teeth showed clearly through the tan of his skin. With determination, Elleah pushed back from his chest, her fingers tingling where they had made contact. His spicy scent mixed with smoke and the not-too-unpleasant odor of seaweed. "Y-yes," she stuttered and cursed her feeble response. Her ankle hurt like hell.

"Listen." He bent close so their noses almost touched. The wave of his hair flopped over his thick brow.

She had the disconcerting urge to brush it back from his temple.

"You're safe."

Funny, this close to him she felt any number of emotions course along her skin and safe was not one of them. "And you would tell a lady otherwise."

He chuckled and the sound pulled a shiver down her spine.

"I simply want to check your injury," he said, voice just above a whisper. "If you try to hobble across the sand, you could actually do it more harm than if we look at it here and now."

How was it possible he was able to make so much sense in the middle of the night? Elleah tried to take his measure. If he were a danger, wouldn't he have already taken advantage? Clearly, he posed no threat, she reasoned. Every fiber of her being screamed otherwise. "Okay," she agreed, reaching to place the tips of her fingers on his arm to hold her balance. "You say you know about these things?"

"I was on the Stanford Rugby team." He smiled and tilted his head to the side.

There was an innocence to the movement and she spread her fingers across his forearm to tighten her grip.

His eyes crinkled at the edge in an endearing way. The concern seemed warm and lost some of its haughty tilt.

"Rugby?"

"We didn't always win."

This was his explanation on his skills in

determining the state of her ankle? Well, what choice did she have? She looked down again at the expanse of sand separating her from the Del, wondering if she should flop down, for grace had surely abandoned her.

He seemed to sense her compliance. With one hand on her elbow, he swung off his jacket and laid it on the sand.

"There's no need—"

With a gentle downward tug of her elbow, he urged, "Sit, just here."

With his assistance, she achieved a seated position and retained some of the little dignity she had left. She complied to his ministrations and straightened her injured leg in his direction. "It's my ankle, I think. I landed funny."

"I didn't laugh."

A giggle escaped before she had time to tamp it down. She enjoyed the speed of his quip. "Nor did I," she returned. How long had it been since she verbally sparred with a man?

He chuckled deep in his throat before kneeling in front of her.

A chill breeze caught her and sent a shiver up her arms where he had most recently held her steady. She had dropped her sweater and couldn't see it in the darkness.

Light fingers moved from the top of her knee down to her foot. Everywhere he touched left a trail of anxious nerve endings. "Permission to remove your shoe?"

Elleah nodded and realized he likely couldn't see. "Y-yes." Then she remembered. "I'm not wearing any." They were likely back with her sweater.

"Well, that helps," he said.

"I think I dropped them." She couldn't go leaving her clothes on the beach. What would management say if they caught her sneaking back to find them in the morning?

"We'll find them in a moment." With a strong hand wrapped around her heel, supporting the weight of her raised calf, he probed the injury, gently moving her foot this way and that. "We haven't moved very far."

When he stretched the limb downward, she suppressed a squeal as the pain shot through her leg.

His fingers pushed against the flesh surrounding the bone. "Your ankle is not broken," he confirmed, raising his gaze to meet hers.

He sounded confident in his diagnosis. His speech was almost hypnotic and seemed to soothe her ache as much as his touch.

"Though you may indeed have some swelling, I'm not feeling any accumulated fluid. I think if I wrap your foot, the binding will see you safely up to the hotel until you can have someone else look at it."

Did he carry spare bandages around with him? His proficiency astounded her. "With what?"

"Excuse me?" With the question, his fingers stilled where they had been massaging the sole of her foot.

She had relaxed into his touch and caressing tones. She longed to lie down and absorb more of his touch. Elleah brought a hand up to brush her hair back from her face where a tendril tickled her cheek. Between his soothing tones and expert touch, her concentration waned.. "What will you use to wrap it?" She fought hard to keep her voice level. "I didn't bring a scarf."

"Yes, well…" He set her foot down upon the sand

and settled back on his haunches.

Through the gloom, she watched him rummage through his pockets, muttering to himself. Glancing out over the ocean, the faint tinge of an indigo line marked the horizon. In a couple of hours dawn would break the horizon. Straining to look anywhere but at her rescuer, she spotted her sweater and shoes a few feet away.

"Aha," he declared and perched back on his knees to lift her calf in his large hand. "My tie."

Elleah swung her gaze back to his. "Your tie?"

"Yes, it'll do for the job." With a practiced ease, he stretched the tie across her calf and wrapped the silky material down and around her ankle—then her foot, leaving her toes exposed. "You won't be able to put your shoe back on."

"I'll ruin your tie if I walk on it."

"I'm not sentimental about ties," he scoffed, flapping his fingers, and smiled up at her.

In the growing light, his grin was even more endearing. Her heart skipped and she wondered what had come over her? She forgot about the throbbing pain in her foot. All of her nerve endings were on high alert craving more of his touch. This was not the haughty neighbor from the morning before. Nor gentleman. This person was a far more dangerous creature. A man in his prime. Being used to boys pretending to be men, Elleah had very little experience from which to draw upon.

He tucked the edge to hold the material in place. "Sacrificed for a good cause." He rolled back on his heels and held out his hand.

Again, with a hand on her elbow and the other at the small of her back, he assisted her to her feet. With the security of the wrap, Elleah was better able to hold her balance.

Once steady, he left her side to retrieve her sweater and sandals clearly visible in the growing light. He laid the sweater over her shoulders and looped the straps over his two fingers. "Here, lean on me." He tucked her hand in the fold of his arm.

The stranger had a panther's stare, and she hesitated. A man like this could threaten everything she vowed to achieve by her independence from her family. She could feel it in the marrow of her being, yet she could no more turn away than she could run on the beach. "Thank you," she said simply, and curled her fingers around his bare forearm. The strength of his bicep offered more security than she was used to receiving.

He bent quickly to retrieve his jacket, giving it a flick across his thigh to dislodge clinging sand before tossing it across his other shoulder.

Keeping her weight to the toes of her foot, she hobbled the vast distance from the water's edge to the boardwalk. Elleah was almost grateful for the ache in her ankle. Concentrating on the pain kept her mind focused and off the man at her side. Had she really been too long out of the company of gentlemen to be so moved by this man?

She heaved an internal sigh at the distance. What had seemed so close a mere hour ago now gave every impression they would never get off the sand.

"Almost there," he said, breaking the silence.

They entered the Del through a side door. The halls were empty. Everyone was still asleep. He stepped behind her when they started up the stairs, and she had the railing for support in the narrow entry. They stopped outside her door.

Elleah lifted her foot and peered at the red-and-blue-striped tie decorated with small anchors. "It may not be ruined," she said, and returned her gaze to his. "I'll have it cleaned."

He grunted and his eyes crinkled. His messed hair looked endearing where it stood up in spots and sprang out over his ears. He swept a hand in dismissal, looking down at her foot. "I'll not miss it."

She drew her key out of her dress pocket, but she didn't turn to the door. She drew in a deep breath, enjoying the closeness and his unique smell. "Thank you."

He tilted his head to the side and the muscle to the side of his strong jaw pulsed.

The movement was as though he were chewing something—pondering a thought—musing before forming the words. Within that moment, he struck her as different than the man he'd been on the beach. His eyes had narrowed, becoming more of a predator. Gone was the gentleman. Here stood a man pondering the situation as one seated at the poker table and weighing his odds.

"I have to say, you're not what I expected." Gone were the gentle tones. He enunciated each syllable precisely.

His words surprised her. She didn't know what he meant.

He cocked his head to the other side and scratched the stubble on his chin. Moving his hand, he cupped her cheek and bent his face to hers. He was now close enough that she could feel his breath slide over her nose. Then he paused, his thumbs stroking a circular motion across her jaw. "Not at all what I expected," he said softly. Then, with the same feather-light touch, he brushed his lips across hers.

Her hands found the contours of his shoulders and she held her balance under the sway of his embrace. With the door to her back, she braced a hip against the jamb.

Hands still cupping her cheeks, he pulled back.

Her breath hitched, lodged in her throat along with any words she may have had.

"I don't normally pay." His fingers continued their mesmerizing strokes and brushed his nose against hers. "But you are a tasty treat. How much?"

Elleah stared into his penetrating gaze. He had eyes the same deep blue of the midnight sky. The lowered lids gave his face a carefree appeal. She tried to comprehend the meaning of his words.

What! Her body stiffened. Surely he hadn't suggested what she thought he had?

Again, he bent and kissed her.

The feel of his mouth moving over hers made her breasts arch toward his touch. "How much?" he groaned against her lips and stepped closer. The swell of his arousal in evidence.

Elleah jumped back, stung, but grateful for the wall holding her upright. "Excuse me?"

He tipped forward, his smile wide. "You'll enjoy yourself, I promise."

Everything she had trusted about him moments before fled. He appeared animalistic—hungry—for her. No. The crack of her palm against the plane of his cheek reverberated off the still walls and echoed down the corridor.

Chapter Five

Reginald woke hours later with a pounding headache, a parched mouth, and weighed down by the smarting of pride. What had he done? He knew what he was thinking, but how had he so misread her? The situation? The opportunity? Or did he?

He ought to forget about the whole sordid event with Miss Jaundoo, but he couldn't. He laid his arm across his face. He couldn't get her wide-eyed look of unfathomable shock from his mind. Then the outraged snap of fire when she slapped him and finally the slamming of her door in his face.

Reginald groaned and banged the cuff of his hand against his brow. But that kiss...those sweet, sensual lips and her rapid response to his touch...how long had it been since he had craved a woman with such a need?

Too long.

Had he ever really craved a woman? He massaged his thumbs in circles against his temples to alleviate the hammering. All of his life, what he wanted he got—a new bike—a vacation—women—the experience of denial annoyed him.

Star-fished across the width of the bed, he kicked the blankets aside and stretched. His back creaked and he sighed. He had to move past this—her—and forget about the whole encounter. Take the name Jaundoo and erase it from his mind. Yet like an itch he couldn't help but scratch, instead of forgetting, he deliberated his reasoning *again*. He'd seen a man—clearly not her husband, leaving her room. Why the pretense? Why allow Reginald to kiss her only to raise a wall of self-righteous indignation when they could have enjoyed quite a memorable interlude?

Rolling over, he looked at the time and grumbled under his breath. He was due down at the marina in less than an hour. The two families—the Burrs and Cavanaughs—were to engage in further bonding, enjoying the yacht Declan secured for the length of their stay. Aside from the beach and sailing, without the office, his secretary, and a phone, there was little else to do to occupy their time. He assumed the ladies also shopped, but he had no interest in that sort of activity. Since his arrival, the men drank any time of the day with Declan being fond of reminding them to hold to east coast time, that way they had a three-hour start.

Reginald was tired of the routine. Again, his neighbor's face swam in front of his eyes. He could think of all kinds of interesting things he could do with Miss Jaundoo to occupy the hours.

"No." The very word hurt his hung-over state. Reginald sat up in bed, dug his toes along the fabric of the carpet, and held his head between his hands.

Regretting a missed opportunity, he slammed his foot on the floor then moaned. The reverberations of impact travelled up all his nerve endings, direct to his squished brain. He continued to rub his temples, hooking his thumbs below his jaw and hearing the scratch of stubble. He positioned the cuffs of his hands over his eyes and bright lights danced behind his lids.

Unable to bear the thought of another grueling day

in the company of people he'd rather not see, he reached for the tumbler on the bedside stand. So much for not drinking. Lifting it to his lips, intent on draining the remainder of the spirit, he paused. Light from the slit in the window coverings glinted off the glass and danced through the liquor. In the honey tones of the liquid, he saw deep green eyes with amber flecks. The smooth skin and pouted lips, aching to be kissed.

Innocent, or seductress? He couldn't decide. His stomach clenched with wanting to feel her touch. The oasis in the desert of nothingness.

"What am I doing?" he mumbled and set the heavy glass back on its perch. This woman had him rethinking his whole plan. "Elleah." Even her name rolled off his tongue like a lover's caress.

Reginald scrubbed his hands through his hair. Surely there were other ways to take over control of the bank without selling his life away? Saddling himself to a woman like Catherine—who did little to rouse his curiosity, never mind his libido—filled him with a sense of dread. Did a career in banking mean the stranglehold noose of a wedding band? "I haven't even walked down the aisle yet, and already I'm turning into *him*."

Twenty minutes later, Declan's distinctive knock pounded on his door and the dreaded *him* entered without waiting for Reginald to answer.

Reginald strode out of the bathroom, towel snug around his hips, hair dripping, and greeted his father with a nod.

"Must you always cut everything to the last minute? The ladies are downstairs in the restaurant, finishing their tea, and you are nowhere to be seen."

41

The thought of food made his stomach roll over. He swallowed back the bile. "As you can see, I am here." Reginald took pleasure in baiting his father.

Declan declined the verbal trap and merely cast him a glowering scowl. There was the face Reginald had come to associate with his father. The friendly, every man façade he had enacted for Peter was growing as old as the charade of potential proposal to Catherine.

"Good morning to you, too." Reginald shook his head and grabbed up his clothes. "Sleep well?"

Declan lit a cigarette and inhaled deeply. "Peter is getting antsy." Declan marched around the room. He strode to the window. With a whistled exhale, smoke billowed from his nostrils and open mouth while he spoke. "We want this deal done. This is my legacy to you." His father cast a quick glance out the window and turned, head encircled by the gray-blue smoke, eyes squinted from the fog. He pointed the cigarette at Reginald. "I know I'm hard on you, and if we didn't need the money to branch out…" He smacked the flat of his other palm against the dresser top. "But we do. And you're ready. You've been ready for a while to take over. Think of it…" A wide grin split the lines of Declan's face. "Ownership over both coasts. The first. We're pioneers in capital."

Reginald picked up his comb from the counter, swept his wayward hair back from his brow, and umm-hummed in response to his father's diatribe.

"Catherine's a good girl," the old man continued. "You know she'll make an excellent wife. She fits in well, socially. She knows the role from accompanying her father."

Reginald tucked his shirt in his crisply pleated

slacks and regarded his father. Yes, he had heard the same tune played many times before. Used to listening without interruption, he hooked his thumbs in the pockets of his pants. Declan had been a hard man to please growing up, but Reginald wouldn't have changed a moment. Life any other way seemed foreign. If he wanted to accomplish even a fraction of the things he envisioned, he needed the backbone and hard shell his father forced him to create.

Turning to the mirror and straightening the buttons of his shirt, Reginald regarded his father through the reflection. Eye-to-eye, he wondered, not for the first time, at his parentage. They bore little resemblance to one another. Of equal height and build, but that was where the family gene pool seemed to branch off. Declan's harsh-boned features always presented a skeletal air, as though the Grim Reaper had laid his cold touch upon him. In this capacity, Declan could silence a room merely by walking in.

Reginald, by contrast, had a banal, devil-may-care demeanor combined with a no-nonsense attitude in his business dealings. He could convince any of their board members to his line of thought without the fear his father created. In his hands, the bank would flourish. Times had changed, and leadership through fear was an outdated notion his father refused to embrace…yet…but he would.

Declan taught him so much and, by watching people's responses, Reginald had learned the rest. How to hold his tongue in a debate and wait for his moment to strike—but never aggressively—no. The best way to have follow-through—leadership from within—was to convince someone it would be in their best interest to agree, as though they had come up with the idea themselves. From Declan, he'd been shown how to school his face into a mask of disregard, to hide his plan, and expose others' weaknesses.

Yes, Declan was correct. Catherine would fit nicely into this game of high stakes, being a woman equally versed in the necessity of rising through the ranks using guile. Money being the grease; brains being the engine.

As he fastened his watch around his wrist, Reginald glanced down and again questioned his motives. Did he really want that—Catherine? Just because this was the life he had grown accustomed, did that mean this life would be enough for him. How about Catherine? Would she be satisfied? Did he have to continue the façade to reach the goal? Was there no other way? Reggie secured his belt through the loop and smiled. "Yes, she would," he said, resuming the thread of conversation.

His father's face lit and he expelled his with a whoosh.

Reggie almost regretted his response—*almost*. "But not for me."

****

Elleah hadn't eaten all day. Every time she thought of eating her stomach heaved as she contemplated how she would get through that evening's show without humiliating herself and the Del who had taken a chance on hiring a no-name to headline their entertainment roster.

In preparation, Elleah selected her dress, a golden crepe that would drape from her waist to heel, and cover her legs entirely to hide the bandage. She picked a pair of cushioned flats designed for walking, not formal wear. Elleah balanced gingerly on her toes, not trusting her ankle to hold up. The shoe fit a little snug over the bandage, but she appreciated the security of the encasement.

Shortly after lunch, the hotel doctor she befriended previously, when he and his wife attended one of her shows, had come by her room and confirmed the ankle was not broken, simply sprained.

Dr. Williams smiled and patted her knee like a grandfather. "I know you won't listen, but I strongly suggest you keep the weight off the injury for a while."

"That will be a little difficult when I have to sing tonight," she replied, adjusting the newly bound bandage to a more comfortable position.

The old man's knees creaked when he bent to the floor to replace his medical supplies in his black bag. "Oh, yes," he responded case in hand. "Well, you can always sit down to sing."

Elleah nodded, noncommittal. If she didn't say, he wouldn't have to object, and by keeping her comments to herself, she avoided having to possibly lie to a kindly old man.

She glanced out the window, gauging the time of day by the angle of the sun. She focused back on Dr. Williams. "You should bring your beautiful bride to the show this evening," Elleah offered. Having met Mrs. Williams first at a small gathering of hotel employees, then several times after at the local market, they had become fast acquaintances. The kindly woman had a mother's air, and Elleah's bruised heart reciprocated willingly.

"Now, there's a thought," Dr. Williams said, pausing by the door, retrieving his hat before fixing the bowler on his head. "She's often saying how I don't take her out enough."

"I could sing a favorite song, if you like," she coaxed and smiled. She left her foot balanced on the stool by her dressing table. "I've been told you're quite the dancer."

"Who told you?" he asked playfully, brows raised. A broad grin lit on the good doctor's features, making him appear years younger and certainly less stern. His eyes crinkled, and he looked aside, lifting one foot then the other in illustration. "I've been known to have a lighter step in my day." With a hand on the doorknob, he cast a quick glance over his shoulder. "That's a good idea. She'd like that very much... Very much indeed."

That had been six-hours ago and still her stomach turned. Between resting her foot in an elevated position, every time she tried to walk, she hobbled at best and hopped the rest of the time. At a snails pace, she covered the distance from her room to the lounge, leaving herself another hour to rest before taking the stage. With a small bit of luck, she'd be able to make it to the stage and get through the night.

Now the moment had come and she had to perform. Elleah tested her weight on her injured ankle and rounded the dais. She spotted the good doctor and his wife, Matilda, in the crowd and focused on them. With controlled movements, she stepped up the two stairs to the small stage and tilted her chin toward the stool.

Dr. Williams smiled and nodded in acknowledgement.

Though the entertainment manager hadn't been pleased by the arrangement, he saw no other means.

One way or another, he needed her to perform. The manager was named Henry. His lipless face folded in on itself in disgust at her injury. He had the mannerisms of an eel—electric—trusting no one and stinging others at every opportunity. Henry made it clear he didn't believe her. "You were hired to keep the men drinking." His diminutive chin disappeared within the collar of his shirt. "How will you manage that sitting down?"

His crassness unnerved her and sent an insulted chill down her spine, making her feel like some whore with a pole and tassels on her breasts. How dare he suggest...but she kept her calm, raised her chin, and remembered her mother's cool demeanor in such circumstances.

"Maybe with the songs I sing." Her response was instant and clipped.

Henry's eyes bulged with her quick response and a vein at his temple throbbed. His reaction gave her motivation. He seemed to think women were to be seen and not heard—that is, unless they were singing for the entertainment of men. The short manager grunted and traced his gaze from the curve of her hips through to the mounds of her breasts. His focus remained trained on the low neckline. "Those are what sell booze," he said with a nod and his prominent nose flared.

His need to have the last word only served to reinforce to Elleah what a small man he was at heart. "Certainly not worth getting aggravated about," she mumbled. In that moment, Elleah weighed what she had run away from versus what she invariably ran to as she watched Henry's face morph from pink, to red, to purple.

In her limited experience, Elleah had found most men expected to say whatever they wanted to a woman without ramifications. Within the confines of her home, growing up, her mother always had a voice in her father's affairs. In fact, the memory gave Elleah pause, remembering her mother and father discussing his banking business and whatever dealings were at the heart of that day's events.

Hearing Arthur's words in her head, she questioned what her parents would think of her performing? She stepped lightly and her ankle smarted. Now was not the time for that kind of pondering.

Elleah turned on the stage, microphone in hand, and regarded the crowd. The inheritance of her father's quick wit was also a blessing in keeping people like Henry in line, reminding them she was not an object, but a person hired to perform as a singer—nothing else. She swept a hand behind her dress to avoid tripping as she assumed her seat on the stool.

Henry stood scowling just inside the drapery to the side of the stage. He had one hand on his hip, the other to his brow shaking his head. Elleah averted her gaze.

Resigned to a situation she could not control, she focused her attention on the crowd and the band. The spotlight illuminated her in a soft circle, and the welcoming applause bathed her with warmth. She took note of the regulars, some of the locals, off-duty hotel staff, and new faces. With a playful air, Elleah swayed her arm at where the band played, and the crowd increased its applause. Following her lead, the conductor and the band began a slow, sultry number.

Unable to resist, Elleah scanned the crowd for *him*. Despite her best efforts, all day she had been on pins and needles, wondering how she would handle the situation when she met *him* again. Considering he lodged across the hall in the hotel, she had no doubt there would be a next time. She tried to block the memory of the sweetest kiss her lips had ever experienced, but even knowing he was a cad did little to erase the tingle of her response.

She had contemplated moving rooms, but her pride held her firm. As the scoundrel, he should be expected to move, not her. Furthermore, should she wish to keep her identity her own, she must also keep her own counsel. Access to money wasn't the issue. The issues would start *if* she did access the available funds, and the resulting questions, queries, and speculation. She needed to avoid such pitfalls.

The conductor gestured at the members of the band as they continued the introduction. With this song, she would normally sway and dance a bit until it came time to sing. Tonight, sitting on her stool, she could do little else but move her upper body and arms as she waited to begin.

Digging her nails into the palm of her hand to keep focus, Elleah had given her head a firm shake when she scanned the hallway before venturing out this evening. Who was this man to hinder her or make her wary? Hadn't she come here for her independence? She had run from two men already; she would not run from a third—a perfect stranger. Or was he? With a kiss that felt so right…an embrace which seemed to suggest so much more…

But he was a stranger. The very nerve of his actions the night before caused her temperature to rise. Why couldn't he have left things at the passion's peak?

Do the gentlemanly thing, take her fingers in hand and kiss the tips before walking away to his room? Certainly they could have picked up the thread of ardor another time. Where had he gotten such ideas? Surely, not all women who sang were also tramps? Certainly, she did not give off such impressions.

The flush heat seared her skin in mortification. Her mother would be so ashamed to imagine a man thought so little of her daughter as to take liberties. Elleah drew a shuddered breath and began her number. After a while, she relaxed into the next piece, smiling at the dancers on the floor and using her hands to sway in time with the beat. By the start of the second set, she felt sure *he* must have indeed checked out of the hotel. Now, she would be left in peace and not have to wonder at his actions or her own lewd temptations. For she had indeed been tempted...by the soft tickle of his whiskers, the feathered brush of his lips. Yes, she would strike the whole incident from her mind for good. Right now. Right after this song, which kept reminding her of his touch and soothing words. Soon. Sometime tonight for sure. She would not wake up tomorrow thinking about *him*.

What had possessed her to allow such a man to kiss her? Never mind. She simply wouldn't let such a thing to happen again. There. Done. The embrace—the kiss—the caress, never happened. But the flutter in her stomach at the thought of his thumb running across her shoulder told her otherwise. To distract her wayward thoughts, Elleah beamed out at the growing crowd, waved, and fluttered her fingers to encourage interaction before leaning to the side table to take a sip from her glass. Replacing the goblet, with one hand and precision of movement, Elleah lifted the skirt of her dress to drape and rearrange it to cover her slippered feet. Mid-motion, her hand froze.

There, across the length of the room, stood the man himself—the object of her obsessive thoughts—leaning casually against a pillar. His right shoulder balanced his weight while he lifted a drink in salute and winked.

Winked.

The nerve!

She let go of the sequined material and her fingers wrapped around the stool. She fought to control the urge to flee. Suddenly, the room seemed too filled with smoke, the air choked with fumes, and the acidic, lingering odor of stale liquor. She couldn't breathe. Her gorge rose and she swallowed convulsively. The music started, and she stared straight ahead, focused on this stranger from across the hallway, unable to remember the lyrics. She opened and closed her mouth, licked her lips, and still nothing emerged.

The bandleader glanced over his shoulder and smiled encouragement.

But the words would not come. She nodded at the conductor and flicked her tongue across her teeth to start singing. She moved the mic up to her mouth, but then she couldn't remember what song to sing. The stream of music was lost to the pounding roar of her heartbeat.

With a raised arm, the band conductor again started from the beginning.

Elleah glanced in horror at the stilled gathering, expectant and waiting for her to begin. Whispered murmurs filled the gaps between notes and her heart hammered. Sweat beaded on her upper lip and she resisted the urge to wipe it away. She returned her gaze to the man who no longer leaned so casually. He stood, and his face wore an expression of concern. Pity? He took a step toward her and, on instinct, she stood and winced with the pain. She would not be pitied.

After another step, he paused.

With his forward motion stilled and the agony of her ankle—like a slap across the cheek—Elleah was restored to the present and picked up the melody.

The band members visibly relaxed and settled back in their seats, while Elleah was left to finish her last set on her injured ankle, pretending all was right in the world. Or as close to right as she could make it—before she met *him*.

Chapter Six

The inky black sky featured a smattering of stars and a quarter moon for illumination. Reginald walked aimlessly around the hotel property, uncaring of where he ended up. Hands deep in his pockets, head bent, shoulders hunched, he tripped over a root, stumbled, missed his step, and fell into the bush as though drunk. If only. "Damn." He grunted. Yes, a couple of stiff drinks might help right at this moment to escape his rampant thoughts.

His shoulder smarted from where he landed in the grass. Managing to pull his hands free of his pockets, he rolled a half turn into a sitting position. Massaging his upper arm, he pondered his circumstances. *How'd this happen?*

Reginald picked a leaf from his hair, then brushed dirt from his sleeve. To say the day had not gone well was an understatement. When had life become so complicated? When had following the rules of the game—the plan as outlined, suddenly become unbearable? When had status lost its quo?

Shaking his head, he berated his sentimentality. Forgetting about his shoulder, he dropped his elbows onto his raised knees, and hung his head, considering.

Surrounded by thick foliage, he leaned back to ponder the heavens. Perhaps illumination would fall down upon him like stardust.

He chuckled. Not stardust—gold sequins, a low neckline, and a soft, rosebud mouth.

Reginald lifted his fingers to his temples and straightened his legs. The answer, it seemed, had jerked him awake with the same harsh crack of the slap across his face from the night before. *She* caused this jolt into reality—the awakening on how he couldn't just take what he wanted. He was accountable. Reginald reverted his position and raised his knees again and hung his head braced between his hands, recalling the instant of change—when he looked in the mirror after his shower and saw his father staring back. That was the moment he decided he would never be that person.

But Declan was having none of it.

Reginald wasn't surprised. Reclining, he leaned back and laced his fingers behind his head, and enjoyed the starry sky. The fresh, leafy green scent surrounding him. He was lost. Not just in his decision-making abilities, but quite literally—physically. He glanced one way and then the other through the bushes. He didn't recognize where he was on the vast property. He sat back up and scanned the darkened landscape. From not too great a distance away, he heard the slap of the ocean surf. The hotel, of course, was at his back, but finding a door to get inside and navigating his return to his own room created a whole other dilemma.

In no great hurry, he relaxed back again. He had nowhere to be, just now. Clouds scuttled across the moon, and Reginald recalled how he had arrived in California intent on following through with his family's wishes. Marry well. Marry money. Create a dynasty and break through the barriers of business banking. He'd trained his whole life for this moment. He had been taught from both parents that marriage, like any contract, was a business arrangement. Why the sudden departure from this line of thought?

Again, the vision of his neighbor, the lovely Miss Jaundoo, scattered his contemplation yet again. Could he really be hung up on an entertainer? Surely not—a lounge singer? His father would definitely follow through on his threats to disown him.

"I might have known," Declan had barked that morning. "Spoiled. That's what you are—spoiled." He paced the room like a caged panther. He lifted the decanter, checked his watch, and then banged the heavy crystal down on the table. "I don't need this right now," he uttered, voice dropping an octave, color dotting his cheeks. "Peter told me over breakfast old Mellon's purchased property in Los Angeles—"

"Not possible," Reginald cut in, stifling the sudden urge to reach for the same decanter. Would his procrastination cost them? The race was on. "The old man's out. You said so yourself. Hasn't been the same since his wife died. And his son…certainly, he's in no position to take control, let alone expand."

To think someone else would have the same ideas of taking control of California banking rooted Reginald to the spot.

Marching to the patio door, Declan threw aside the curtains and lit a cigarette, sucking the smoke into his lungs with a deep, audible inhale. "I'll not stand by and watch what I have taken a lifetime to build thrown away over cold feet." The older man stared intently back at Reginald.

Able to read his father's thoughts, Reginald waited for the explosion, holding his comments.

Declan dragged so deeply on the cigarette, in a moment he held a cylinder of ash. Finally, releasing the smoke, he said, "I think you're right, though. Mellon's washed up. I don't know what the purchase means, but I hardly think he's in a position for expansion."

Reginald's hadn't realized his pulse had quickened until that moment when his heart resumed a more pleasant beat. "We ought to have Gregory snoop around, just in case."

"Agreed." Declan stood on the divide between the room and the balcony. "Now, about Catherine."

More confident in his decision than a moment before, Reginald adopted a more casual air and resumed dressing. "Is Peter the only backer, or is he simply the most convenient?" Could there be a way out by steering Declan toward another potential family?

"Aside from the obvious fact that you do indeed know Catherine, and she is familiar with our family."

Reginald's fingers paused. A flushed crept up his neck. "Aside from that, yes." Could he avoid the trap of marriage?

His father turned to face him, disgust lighting his features. Declan's cheeks puffed and glistening with moisture. "No, I won't do it. I won't stand by and allow you to throw it all to the four winds. I would sooner sell everything to Peter and be done with banking altogether than let you tarnish our good name. The marriage is understood—it's been understood for quite a while now...this union *will* take place." He paused to catch his panting breath. "For you to breach contract..."

Reginald's hope sailed away on the breeze that scooped the cigarette smoke out the door. Then Declan's words faded, lost in the same rant Reginald had heard too many times, for far too long.

There in the bushes, back in the moment contemplating the heavens, darkness coated him like oil, and he didn't know if he would rather stay obscured in the shadows or rise and find his way to his room. Reginald flopped a hand across his chest, defeated. He understood his father's position. Hell, it had been him who first spotted the opportunity when he conceived what he wanted to do with the bank—once it was his. He positioned the offering, set all the cogs in motion, used all of his skills, made his father believe it was his idea, and now?

Breathing deeply, Reginald tried to rationalize a solution. Out of the darkness, the strings of timeless Bach floated around him and lulled his aching mind. Comforted by the string and wind instruments, only after a few moments did he realize the melody came from without, rather than from within his own head.

He glanced up and behind. Above, many terraces dotted the side of the building. He stood, brushed off his pants, and slapped his palms together to rid them of the dust. Tired of wandering, he wished he knew where he was. Exhausted, he craved his bed. With a drink—or two—he could slip into oblivion. There would be a welcome occupation.

He stepped back to the path and directed his gaze to the backlit figure silhouetted on the first veranda.

His imaginings became a reality as he recognized the entertainer—the singer. Hair loose about her shoulders, she was clad in the silk robe he'd admired so much the other morning. With the light funneled from the doorway, her shape became easily discernable through the thin fabric. The curve of her hip, the angle of her leg where her knee bent so her foot could rest on the small step, oh, and the swell of her breasts as she swayed to the music. His palms tingled with the memory of what that sway felt like when he assisted her off the beach.

While he spied, transfixed, she hobbled back through the doorway, and he ached for her limp. His thumb brushed the tips of his fingers, remembering the smooth calves when he'd wrapped her injury. How could he have been such a fool? Was she a missed opportunity? Reginald had the feeling what he wanted—needed from Miss Jaundoo—couldn't be taken; only she could give it.

He lowered his head and brushed fingers through his hair, lifting the flop off his brow. Squeezing his eyes shut he tried to block the memory of her soldiering through her performance. What pain she must have experienced earlier that very evening, standing on the sprained ankle and singing with the sweetness of a songbird without a care in the world. He knew very well the opposite was true.

The fading music from her veranda stopped and, after a pause, started again. She must have turned the record over. He returned his gaze to the hotel and waited, heart pounding with anticipation of seeing her come again through the doorway and onto the veranda where he could admire her from a distance.

Reginald wondered at the assumptions he'd made about the lovely Miss Jaundoo. Was he wrong in thinking she was simply decoration for the most profitable man in the audience on any given night? Clearly—or else he wouldn't be standing here right now, contemplating what she wore under that slip of a robe—if anything. His loins swelled considering the latter. Taking a few steps down the path he considered leaving, then shaking his head, returned.

Tonight offered even more curiosity. What kind of jazz singer listened to Bach? Or spoke with such a cultured accent? Certainly none of the women he was familiar with. He grimaced, releasing a small groan of disgust. There had been his first mistake, assuming she was anything like the women he knew from the New York lounge scene. On reflection, he remembered her reaction, tone, and choice of words when she tripped over his sleeping form. Had he not had so much to drink and his wits been about him, he may not have made such a ghastly mistake. Perhaps he could have wooed her into his bed.

A wry smile curled his lip, and he lifted a hand to his bristled cheek. He thought not.

He took a step closer, wondering if she would come back. In attending the show this evening, he hadn't meant to scare her. That, more than anything else, bothered him. Her reaction had been instantaneous. Upon spotting him, her smoldering gaze, usually lost in the melodies of her songs, widened instead, focusing on his. Panic and trepidation filled their depths. If he were correct in his earlier assumptions about the slight Jaundoo, he wouldn't have recognized the alarm in her enlarged eyes earlier. Instead, he would have received what he had come to expect from the seedier side of his life—a coy smile, something to indicate her rejection of his advances the night before had been part of the greater charade to gain his interest, to create pursuit. Sometimes even a wink to encourage further advances. But this obviously had not been the case, and now he was fully aware of his mistake.

Reginald paced back and forth, hands on his hips. How long would he wait staring up from ground level to the balcony in some Romeo pose waiting for a Juliette who wanted nothing to do with him? At least a few more minutes. He caught his breath when she returned to the railing. Her hands hung loose over the side while her face tilted to the stars.

What would she be thinking as she contemplated the heavens? He couldn't distinguish her features, but he imagined a slight smile. He wanted to think of her happy, not morose, as he had seen her the first morning, or anxious like earlier in the evening. Instead, he pictured her face as it was when she was lost in the harmony of her music. Color high, she seemed to breathe the very notes she sang. If the famous composer Bach had had this woman around, all of his music would have included vocals to accompany the composition.

Devil be damned by the plans he made in New York. Here in California all of those schemes seemed to wash away on the tide. He walked closer to a flowering tree and leaned against the thick trunk. A longing filled his heart. Reginald wanted to stand by her side, conversing about the stars, pointing out the constellations above. He yearned to have those unique green eyes fasten upon him and smolder with the passion she exuded when she sang. Imagining her body, a well-strung instrument, he craved the ability to elicit an opus from her soul.

"Who's there?" a deep male voice barked across the expanse of lawn. "This is private property. There under the tree…you…what are you doing loitering around here?"

Reginald squinted against the glare of the flashlight intruding on the dreamlike quality of the evening's darkness. He glanced up at the balcony in time to see her grip the railing and peer through the gloom in his direction. His voice caught in his throat, preventing him from answering and revealing himself.

Then, she stood straight and limped back into her room. The sharp sound of the door sliding home ended the tranquility of the symphony and brought him back to the present but no closer to resolution.

Chapter Seven

What started as a hobble had eclipsed, fortunately, into a slight limp over the morning of pacing her room, brooding, like a caged tiger. So much for resting. The four beige walls shrank in on Elleah, creating a claustrophobia. Even the view from the balcony held little appeal when she could only look out over the lush scenery, instead of enjoying strolling through the beautiful gardens.

With a huff, she slumped into the chair in front of her dressing table. She rearranged the application tools and makeup, selected a vial of perfume, examined the bottle and set it back down. "This is stupid," Elleah told her reflection in the mirror and pulled a face. With harsh strokes, she dragged the brush through her hair. "You didn't come here to hide."

After a full exhale, she inhaled slowly through her nose, then puffed out her cheeks, creating a sputter through her lips. She smiled, recalling how her grandfather would make the very same sound and imitate an elephant, waving his arm in front of his face like the trunk to get her and Arthur laughing. The memory softened her demeanor. Using a gentler hand, she smoothed her hair before braiding the long strands to curve around the nape of her neck and fall over her shoulder. Somewhat calmer, she shuffled to the bathroom to wash and freshen her face.

Recalling a favorite song she planned to incorporate into her act, she hummed as she walked to the closet. She ran a hand down her neck, from her jawline to her breastbone contemplating her wardrobe. Casting a quick glance outside, she chose a rose-colored shift dress with a petal-designed shawl. Testing her weight on her injured ankle, she decided, for the limited distance she planned to walk, she would be fine.

Besides, anything's better than these four walls.

The good doctor may disagree, but Elleah decided the sprain was all but healed. Occasional hobble, she covered the distance from closet to bed and back again. She really could walk now without cringing. Today was her first day without a scheduled show in a long while, and she'd be damned if she would concern herself with *him*—her arrogant neighbor from across the hall—and miss out on wandering through the market stalls.

Grabbing her handbag, she noticed his tie lay neatly pressed on her dresser table. She contemplated returning it to him. Perhaps she should leave it hanging on his doorknob? Or she could simply toss it away. Picking it up, her fingers traced the intricate design within the soft silk. No, she couldn't do it. The price of this Hermes tie could feed a typical family for a week, and she wouldn't throw it away. Maybe she could give it to someone. *No*…she placed it back on the bureau.

"Enough." She strolled to the door and opened it. Pausing, she glanced back at her tidy room, through the balcony door and the golden sunshine beyond. The day beckoned and she wouldn't waste one more minute pondering that cad of a man. Hand on the knob, she strode across the threshold and closed her door with a decisive click. With as much grace as she could muster, she marched down the hallway toward the exit.

After two hours of browsing the market stalls, checking out local wares, Elleah's ankle was a little worse for wear. Keeping her weight on the toes of her right foot, she made her way back along the boardwalk, strolling slowly. Despite her discomfort, she didn't regret the sojourn to the bazaar. Full of bright-colored fabrics, flowers, scents, and food, she'd accomplished her goal. Besides, she had definitely needed the escape, if only from her own wandering thoughts. Hungry, but emotionally better, carrying a brightly designed cloth shopping bag with a new dress and shoes to match, she ambled into one of the four hotel restaurants. The Water's Edge restaurant was her favorite for its view of the beach and expanse of ocean beyond. The coastline of Mexico offered a purpled silhouette to the left of the horizon. Chatting with the various vendors, for a short time at least, she had managed to block the image of *him*—those intense eyes and his blunt, cleft chin with a scratch of stubble.

Now, back at the Del, the memory of his light touch with those strong hands sent a delicious chill down her spine. How long had passed since she was courted properly? *Too long*. But hadn't that been one of the reasons she had fled New York—to avoid the projected matrimony to a man of her father's choosing? The strangulating noose of a husband only interested in the position she could offer at her father's bank. And, not to be forgotten, fulfilling societal expectations.

Not for the first time in the last while, Elleah wonder what had she escaped, really? From the frying pan into the fire, as her mother would say. In her present circumstance, she was prey to a daily dose of hungry gazes. Surrounded by men who saw her as an ornamental object they wanted to possess. And these were not the gentlemen of ballrooms where rules were followed—these were the power-hungry businessmen here to stake a claim in the wild west. Where was the difference between this and the social climbers? Elleah shook her head unable to find the same spark of indignation that had prompted her to flee New York and the trappings of expectations.

She hadn't so much as found out his name—her neighbor from across the hall. What kind of man didn't introduce himself? Yet, when he had helped her on the beach, she thought he was different. With his gentle touch and caring tone—the magic of the beach, the tilt of the moonlight, and the music of the surf. By the time they arrived at her room, she was ready to accept him as different, and then...

She was tired of replaying the scene—she as the tart and he as the everyman.

Spotting an open table, Elleah maneuvered through the crowd, sending a smile to the server. Grateful to finally be able to sit down, she huffed, tossed her bag on the empty seat, and sat at her usual spot on the patio. Nodding at Jacques, the maître d', she glanced at the menu. The words blurred in her renewed humiliation. How could she have allowed such a thing? Her cheeks burned recalling how she returned the kiss of a man whose identity remained a mystery.

"Miss Jaundoo," Jacques' smooth tones caressed as he approached the corner table. "Don't you look lovely this afternoon?"

Elleah folded the menu and laced her fingers to rest on the tabletop. She smiled up at the handsome

Mexican and, not for the first time, wondered about what his real name was. His midnight back hair was greased back from his broad forehead and accentuated his high cheekbones. The full moustache and thick brows took on a life of their own when he grinned, giving him an almost comic air. "We've a nice, crisp house white featured today. A local vineyard."

"Local? Really?" Elleah had heard the California winemakers were making quite a name for themselves. Not new to winemaking, they tended to more regional recognition than global. Nobody could fault the Californian ambition, much more stoic in their pursuits than the New Yorkers to whom she was accustomed. She nodded at Jacques' apparent pride.

"A Sonoma from a mission just outside San Diego. A rival for any French or German import."

"Really?" Elleah grinned skeptically. "I'm feeling adventurous. I'll give it a try."

"You won't be disappointed." The stout man hurried away, intent on his task, and returned almost as quickly, the recently uncorked bottle folded within a stiff red napkin. A whisper of fog wafted from the open neck. He poured a mouthful into the gleaming crystal and offered Elleah the first taste.

Lifting the glass just under her nose, she breathed deeply of the aroma. She spun the liquid within the goblet watching the liquid catch the glint of light. Sipping, she drew the liquid between her lips into the warmth of her mouth, allowing the cool sensation to wave across her palate, coaxing it from cheek to cheek, before swallowing. The bouquet of rose, honey, and a hint of oak cascaded down her throat, leaving a wake of infinite pleasure. "Jacques." She beamed, genuinely impressed. "Lovely."

"Of course," he agreed and bowed his head in gracious acceptance of his expertise. Then his dark eyes focused on her. "Will you partake the chef's masterpiece?"

"As you recommend." She swirled the wine, enjoying the prism of color. Taking a moment to contemplate, she held the wineglass at arm's length to enjoy the view of the beach through the crystal. If only she were versed in photography, the image would create a lovely picture. Her stomach growled in anticipation of the meal to come. Every day since her arrival she'd had the chef's pick and had yet to be disappointed. "It's not too early?"

"Never for you, madam."

The meal arrived without delay and Elleah took her time enjoying every mouthful. Absorbed in the deliberation of the feast before her, the vintage, and the roll of the surf in the distance, Elleah was startled out of her trance by the boisterous guffaws of the party just inside the restaurant. By the sounds of things, the people were gathered for a celebration. A wedding? Perhaps an engagement—whatever it was, the Del was certainly the perfect setting. The descending sun had highlighted the azure blue sky with streaks of pink and orange. Fishing boats, darker shadows cutting through the white-tipped waves, moved through the water on their way back to port.

Elleah stood and retrieved her bag from the next seat. After a day of activity, she felt significantly better than she had that morning. Pleasantly tired and ready to rest. Perhaps she could put the whole unfortunate event—with *him*—out of her mind now. Their liaison was, after all, over and done with. She hadn't even laid eyes on the man all day.

When she stood, her shawl slipped off her shoulder and she twisted to grab an end and fold it within the curve of her arm. In mid motion, she caught sight of *him* on the inside of the glass-windowed wall. His profile was sideways to her, standing and addressing the table of five. To his right sat a straight-laced, austere woman of the approximate age as Elleah, the cream of her pale complexion just visible under her fashionable hat. Elleah watched as the woman looked up with an adoring gaze at *him*—her *him*.

"Enough of the preamble," barked a large, older man seated directly opposite. "Get on with it, Reginald. I'm an old man, have some mercy."

Reginald. The name suited.

Without consideration, Elleah took a hesitant step forward, not wishing to be spotted, but curious.

Reginald picked up the young woman's hand and bent to kiss the tips of her fingers.

Elleah recognized the soft touch. Hadn't he used those same hands on her to soothe and comfort her after her fall on the beach?

To Elleah, his gaze seemed to search the pale face of this other woman as though seeking inspiration for words that wouldn't find their way out of his lips. Her imagination played out a familiar scene, she as the other woman—the harlot—and the fair lady, his wife. My God, what had she done? What had she allowed herself to be part of? Heat flooded her face, black spots danced before her vision and her knees felt like they would be give way. The meal so recently enjoyed, danced back up her throat, threatening. She swallowed and squeezed her eyes closed.

"Catherine," Reginald said with a smile that didn't crinkle his eyes. "We've known each other most of our lives."

Elleah took another step and reached for the edge of a chair to maintain her balance. *Is she his wife?* Had he kissed her—propositioned her—and he was already married? Had he truly imagined her a whore? She was rocked to her core to conceive someone had made such an assumption about her character.

"From middle school hijinks to college escapades, we have always made time for each other."

No, by God, this was a proposal. She gripped the edge of the chair, her knuckles white. Firming her spine, she strove to control the dizziness and concentrated on her next move. Elleah tore her gaze away and focused on the exit. A few more steps would take her to the boardwalk entrance and away from this farce. Again, her shawl slithered from her shoulders, and as she reached for it she collided with a waitress darting between tables on her way to the kitchen. "Oh, I'm so sorry," Elleah gushed and moved forward as quickly as she could.

"One moment, miss," the waitress called after her. "Your bag."

Elleah glanced behind and realized she had indeed only taken her purse. Her shopping bag sat abandoned on the chair. Covering a groan, she stepped back onto the patio and made the mistake of glancing back to the windowed wall.

There he stood tall, facing her. He stared openly at her, mouth slightly parted.

His frank appraisal caused a tingle of sensations to

ride her spinal cord. Her heart thudded against her ribs and again, blackness danced at the edge of her vision. She had to escape at once.

Everyone at his table now glanced in her direction.

Tearing her gaze from the lovely couple, Elleah accepted the bag from the waitress with a nod and muttered thanks. She turned and fled the area as quickly as her injured ankle would carry her. Once she rounded the corner of the building, she slowed her pace and deepened her shallow breaths.

A strong grip on her arm brought her up short.

Chapter Eight

Reginald dropped Catherine's fingers from his own and quickly shuffled through the tables of the restaurant, past the glass doors and out of the building. With a hurried step, he rushed to the boardwalk where he paused to look for the woman he couldn't escape, even in his dreams since meeting her.

Heart pounding, he walked one direction, then another, catching a glimpse of a hobbling figure in the crowd. Before he had time for further contemplation of his actions, Reginald caught up to her in a matter of moments. His need to apologize for his behavior burned like acid in his stomach. He didn't know what had caused him to make such an assumption—well, he did, but he wasn't proud of the way he had so quickly jumped at the notion—and seeing how frightened she was whenever she caught sight of him knotted his gut. No mater what the outcome, he could fix this—he would fix this—now.

His fingers grasped her upper arm and her step faltered. Thinking she may tumble over, he reached for her other shoulder and held her facing him. He wanted to say something—anything, but the sight of her, her body so close to him, words failed. Smoothing his palm along her shoulder to reach behind her neck, he pulled her to him and kissed her. Her mouth fit his warm and moist. She tasted of sunshine and fresh wine. He pulled back, nose close to hers and smiled.

Her large eyes consumed her face, and she twisted out of his grasp. "What do you want?" she hissed. Her gaze searched behind him and color flooded her smooth cheeks.

"I want…" He hesitated. Where were the words?

She hobbled back a step. "Yes?" She crossed her arms across her chest.

"I want…"

She widened her stance as though preparing for battle. She filled the gap. "I understand you want." She flung an arm back to the restaurant. "Everything, it seems."

"No, no." He looked down at the uneven wooden planks and shook his head, confused. What was wrong with him? *Apologize and get it over with.* "I want…I want…to know who you are." *What?*

She uncrossed her arms and her fingers tightened into fists. Would she slug him?

"Who I am?"

Her voice had risen and an incredulous note touched the octave. Her face pinched, and she squinted against the glare of the sun. She wasn't wearing a hat to shelter her from its direct impact. Her mouth opened and closed several times before she finally licked her lips, her hands opening revealing her palms turned upright toward him.

"Elleah Jaundoo."

He noted how her last name was spoken with a foreign accent.

She extended her hand. "And you are Reginald…?"

The question hung a fraction longer than necessary.

He fought the urge to take her hand, pull her to him, and kiss her again.

"Cavanaugh," he answered and accepted her small hand in his. He resisted the impulse to trace a finger along her palm, such was the impact of even mild contact. Her smooth, soft hand belied a firm grip. He cleared his throat. "Nice to finally meet you."

Her face split into a smile and a chuckle bubbled up to be released on a breathy sigh. She raised a handkerchief to her lips in a delicate manner. She dabbed her lips, chin, and brow before replacing the slip of cloth within the confines of her purse. Her mouth thinned. "I'm sure your *fiancée* will be missing you." She raised her chin to point back along the boardwalk.

"I'm sure." Reginald reached for her hand, wanting to explain, but she pulled back. He dropped his arms back to his sides and shook his head, completely unsure about what he was doing. "But, I want to—"

"More wants," she added, her voice biting.

He couldn't help the smile and brushed fingers through his hair. She was a woman who couldn't be taken; she must be earned. He knew that now. "I owe you an apo—"

Cool fingers curved over his shoulder. Their chill permeated through the cotton of his shirt. "Reggie?" Catherine's clipped step paused at his back. "Is everything okay?"

He turned midway and glanced at the willowy woman, so lacking in any curves. His gaze traced a path down to her hand, which had slipped down on his upper arm. He lifted his vision to lock with Catherine's, but her stare didn't change even when she uncoiled her fingers from his arm. How different she was from the entertainer, with her feisty expressions and spitfire body. With features so bland, only Catherine's voice held any interest, and its nasal, elongated east-coast pronunciations grated at the best of times.

He couldn't escape the flutter in his gut. Here he stood at the fork in the road, choosing which way to turn. He cast his gaze between the two very different women. One who would have him despite his chasing after another woman and one who drew him to her and demanded he be better than himself. At this moment, he could please his father and become a replica of the old man—a carbon copy of so many in their social circles, or he could break out of the mold and be a man this woman—this singer had shown him the briefest glimpse.

With a single stride, he distanced himself from Catherine's cool gaze, out of arms reach to stand beside Miss Jaundoo. "Everything is fine, Catherine. I'll be back in just a moment."

Catherine's thin lips firmed and all but disappeared in her face. He knew his abrupt tone smarted, but to Catherine's credit, she didn't back down. A line formed between her brows and through her narrowed gaze, he could read the fleeting thought of her being so close to the prize now, she wouldn't stand aside at this point. Reginald quite literally felt the archer's marks painted on his chest. Had he any doubt of his decision before, his stomach settled and he breathed easier. The choice was made.

"And your friend?" Her chin rose a fraction in Elleah's direction. "Will you introduce us?"

"Of course." He moved to the side so the two

women faced one another. "Catherine, you likely recognize Miss Jaundoo from the hotel—"

"Ah, yes, the lounge singer," Catherine sneered, drawing out the words.

Catherine's distaste was as evident as vinegar on her palate. Her pointed nose lifted a fraction and she used her height to boldly stare down at Elleah.

Reginald resisted the urge to cut Catherine down verbally. Instead, he drew a deep breath and swept a hand toward Elleah. "Miss Jaundoo…" Reginald moved his focus from Elleah to Catherine. "May I present Catherine Burr, from the Burr Family Banks of Massachusetts."

Elleah didn't respond immediately. With precise movements, she adjusted her shopping bag in the crook of her arm and took hold of her purse with the same. She stood still, yet she seemed to grow in height. Her strong chin lifted and a frosty smile barely lifted her cheeks, which had gone pale.

She held her fingers out in greeting. "Nice to meet you—"

"His fiancée," Catherine cut in and ignored the petite woman's outstretched hand. She tucked her gloved hand in the bend of his elbow and forcibly turned him back to the hotel. "Our families are waiting. We really must be getting back."

Reginald had very rarely found himself at such a loss. Loss of words—lost as to what to do next, but he did know he would not be maneuvered. He made his choice. With a mental nod to reinforce his decision, he firmed his lips and dug in his heels to prevent Catherine from dragging him away. To combat his rising uncertainty, he patted her hand. "You go on to the restaurant and tell them I will be there momentarily."

For the first time in their 'courtship', though he was sure it would not be the last, he saw Catherine's eyes flash with blue fire and her normally bland expression changed into one of haughty determination. Her thin brows rose and the smile reminded him of a head master he'd had at private school—the forerunner of a strap should he not obey. She glanced at Elleah and then into his face, searching for an answer he wouldn't give.

"Are you sure?" Her voice held a trace of warning.

He released her fingers from his grasp. "Go on." He gave a nod to the large red-roofed building. "I'll be but a minute."

Air whistled past her thin lips, her shoulders rose then fell, while her feet came together with a near click of her heels. "What business could you possibly have—"

Reginald had had enough. Despite the slither of snakes in his gut and the revived hammer of his heart against his chest, he laid a palm on each of her shoulders and turned her back toward the hotel. "I'll be but a minute." He firmed his tone and bent slightly in her direction.

Her face fell into its usual dull expression of a placated horse.

Glancing over her shoulder, she nodded at Elleah then returned her gaze to Reginald. "Yes…well…shall I order you a coffee, Reggie?"

He released his hold on her and moved a hand to the small of her back. The knot in his stomach loosened. With minimal pressure, he pushed with the tips of his fingers. "Please, do."

For a long moment, Reginald watched Catherine walk away, her progress measured and precise. He turned to face Elleah, intent on making a proper apology, but she, too, had walked off in the opposite direction. Her step, however, was halted and lopsided. He supposed she had been too long on a recovering injured ankle. Within a few paces, he had caught up. He reached for her arm, thought better of his actions and dropped his arm to his side.

"I would prefer if you let me be," she whispered without making eye contact. "You have involved me in a compromising situation whereby your fiancée has now made assumptions about my character."

Her words made him wonder again about who she was. The situation she described so reminded him of his sister, his step faltered. Going against the accepted road his parents had laid out for her, Maribel had rebelled, determined to continue her liaison with a married mam, until Declan had her institutionalized. Maribel's situation was a tragedy. He regretted not being man enough to stand beside her.

The women he met in the New York jazz scene very rarely considered their conversations with men compromising, and certainly wouldn't give two scraps about what his supposed fiancée thought. At the same time, he would never have considered the same within proper society, which is why, until this very moment, he had agreed with Declan's decisions regarding Maribel. He shook his head, and gnashed his teeth, stunned at his own rapid thoughts.

With every step, however slow, Reginald moved away from the path of acceptable behavior. He would forge his own future. "She has made assumptions on a few things today," he muttered. "And I must apologize."

"Accepted," Elleah returned briskly and continued to march on.

Her stiff posture and regal bearing pegged her as unusual. There could be no doubt in his mind she was not what she seemed. He kept pace with her easily enough.

She glanced across at him. Moisture brimmed in the corner, making her eyes bright. Color splotched her pale cheeks. "Please, leave me in peace."

"Stop." He reached for her arm.

She wrenched away her arm. "I must get back."

His fingers curled into his palm. "Get back to what?"

"That is none of your concern."

He slapped his fist into his palm. "I am concerned." He reached for her wrist, halting her progress. "There has been a misunderstanding."

"I think not," she flared, the splotch of color spread across her cheeks. Stray tendrils of hair broke free of the plait and laced across her brow and face. "You are the worst possible man ever, not fit to call yourself a gentleman. Y-you have a fiancée—"

"She is not—" The flash of Catherine's face enraged him. The snakes that tangled in his gut, curled, and he stiffened his spine. That woman would never be his bride.

"Not what?" Elleah shot, chin held high, pulling on the wrist he would not relinquish.

"She is not my fiancée."

Elleah threw her head back and laughed a sound made foreign in its ferocity. "Huh, you may want to inform Miss Burr of the Burr Family Banks of Massachusetts." She straightened her stance and glared at Reginald. Her brows shot up into her hairline in an expression of total disbelief. "I saw you."

Reginald sighed and swept his free hand through his hair to rest behind his neck where it remained while he considered a strategy. How could he make Elleah comprehend something for which he didn't yet have an understanding? All he knew was his attraction to this petite singer whose evocative voice had drawn him from the water's edge to seek her out. A woman to wake him from the slumber of acceptance into a life of choice. "Yes, well…it's a long story."

She shook her head and altered her gaze to take him in from head to toe. "I'm sure."

"I want to apologize." His voice had risen and he slapped a hand to his forehead. Removing his palm, slowly down to his side, he stared into the depths of her green eyes, wondering why he felt so compelled to chase this woman. Why explain? He'd never had to explain before. Clarity compelled him.

He understood the consequences of these actions, yet he wouldn't be stopped. From his father's wrath to Catherine's scorn, this one move had the potential to possibly ruin any chances to create the dynasty he originally envisioned.

"You already did."

He softened his tones. "No, not that." He smiled, aching with a tenderness to caress her cheek. "Well, not *just* that. For the other night."

Her brows formed a V over her nose, and she altered her gaze. "Nothing happened."

He lifted his shoulders only to let them sag. "I

acted the cad, and I am sorry. I'd had too much to drink, passed out on the sand, and was not in my right frame of mind…" He swept a palm expansively toward the beach. "Family pressure—business dealings, just so much going on, decisions needing to be made, and I…you wouldn't understand."

She shook off his grasp, succeeding in releasing her wrist. "Clearly," she returned and took the stray tendril of hair and tucked the strand behind her ear. She hobbled a few steps, muttering, "What would an entertainer know of important business decisions? But—" She whirled around to face him. "You forget. I don't care. You helped me, and for that I am grateful. And that is that. We are done. We are not involved. Until today, I didn't even know your name. You need not concern yourself with me. I accept your apology, and you can get back to your…your fiancée."

"She's not…" But his words floundered on the rising wind as Elleah moved farther out of his reach.

****

Reginald shuffled his feet, but let her go. Walking in slow motion, he retraced his steps back to the restaurant. Only his father remained, drink in hand, face suffused in anger.

"What has happened to you?" Declan barked. "You are about to throw away all we have worked for over a piece of skirt who can sing."

If there had ever been a time when his father could relate, that time had long since past. Declan seemed no more capable of experiencing the closeness with another person beyond the boardroom and business dealings than a whale had of growing legs and walking along the beach. Reginald sighed. "She's not a piece of skirt, as you say. It's not like—"

His father grabbed him by the arm and led him out of the building and beyond earshot of anyone interested in listening.

Once outside, Reginald shook off his hold and continued on his own toward the boardwalk, until he reached the benches. Storm clouds had begun to gather on the horizon and the few people left on the beach were a ways away. The smell of rain blew in off the sea. He drew a bracing breath and turned to face Declan.

Declan pointed a finger and pushed it into Reginald's chest. "Skirt or not, by God, it had better not be like that!" His father's face was puce. The vein along his temple bulged and throbbed and the wind lifted the hank of hair covering his receding brow. "You were so close and then…and then…what exactly happened?"

Reginald crossed his arms over his chest. "I had an encounter with the woman—"

"An encounter? What kind of encounter?" Declan's chest rose and fell with shallow breaths. His eyes bulged and with expert precision he drew a cigarette from its silver monogramed case within his shirt pocket and lit the fag with a matching lighter.

Reginald resisted the urge to strike the lit stick from Declan's mouth and wipe the foul thoughts so evident on his father's features. "Not like what you are imagining." Out of habit, for want of something to do besides talk to the old man, Reginald longed for a drink. The beach bar sat within walking distance and he started to stride toward it; with enough booze would mean oblivion, but then stopped. He would not submit to the self-medication in which Declan indulged. Instead he turned to face his father. "I had to apologize for a misunderstanding."

"A misunderstanding?" Declan's brow furrowed. He drew so deeply on his cigarette it all but disappeared in a puff of smoke. "What kind of misunderstanding? You are leaving a lot out of the conversation. Did you bed the girl? Do we have to worry about an unfortunate side effect to this impulsive…"

Reginald dropped his arms to his side, then raised them to the sides of his head. Lowering his head and squeezing his eyes shut, he stamped his foot in the sand. "No, of course not—"

"What do you mean, of course not?" Declan dropped the spent cylinder of ash in the sand and stamped his heel on top of it, mashing it into the ground. He raised his gaze to his son.

"I mean, nothing happened." Reginald huffed, marched back to the bench, and threw himself onto the bench. He straightened his legs and crossed his ankles, dropping them down to the sand. "A simple misunderstanding. I apologized and it's over."

Declan had followed him to the bench, but stood. The old man's penetrating ice blue stare sizzled through Reginald, seeking the truth of the matter.

"Your antics created quite a wedge. Peter was prepared to come to blows over the matter this afternoon, had it not been for Catherine herself calming the situation. You know Mellon is close and has purchased a building? And now this."

Reginald sat up straight, uncrossed his ankles and leaned his elbows on his knees. "What? Who?"

"I told you," Declan continued and lit another

cigarette. His gray complexion matched the spent ash. "Mellon was in Los Angeles, and Greg confirmed he has indeed bought a building downtown in what is a budding financial district."

"Mellon?" Reginald grabbed his head in his hands. They'd been warned, but he hadn't taken it seriously. How could he? This was their plan. They had planned to buy in that area, which was perfectly located to industry, shipping, and commercial business. In combination with the potential loss of Peter's backing, this would be disastrous. The full measure of his actions weighed down upon him like the clouds closing in off the horizon. "Gerard Mellon?"

Declan flapped a hand and turned to face the beach. "Have we any other immediate rivals?"

Reginald stood and joined his father. "You told me he wasn't an issue. You were sending Greg to investigate only as a matter of formality."

The powerhouse that had once been Gerard Mellon had died with his wife. Reginald's investigation into their competition confirmed this before he had ever approached Declan with this idea that had now imploded his actions. He placed his hands on his hips and searched for answers in the pattern of the growing waves. "Greg's been known to overreact before. Is he sure about this? You confirmed my initial understanding that this would be nothing."

Reginald paused to draw breath. Everything had changed so quickly. "When we discussed this, and I mentioned Gerard's lack of play this last year, you said his son, Arthur was too young to take over, and the man himself hasn't been the same since losing his wife."

"Turns out you and Mellon's boy are of the same

age. The young Mellon is twenty-eight and given Greg's report, the situation is significantly worse than we first imagined." Back to business now, Declan's face reverted to its normal hue, and they returned to the bench. "Greg confirmed. Arthur, actually finalized the real estate deal in Los Angeles a month ago. Even before we started scouting. Apparently, they had other business out here—"

"What other business?" Reginald sat straight, ready to sprint. If ever there was a time for a drink. He ached for something to do with his hands other than to curl them into impotent fists. How he longed to hit something, release some of his pent-up frustration. Instead, he waited, dreading the words which would tell him his chances of running the bank the way he dreamed were over.

Declan's voice hardened and he lifted a palm to illustrate a sweep of the general area. "Greg's sources tell him Gerard's given Arthur full autonomy to move forward with a branch out here. The old man—"

Reginald arched an eyebrow and chuckled without humor. "He's younger than you—"

Declan rolled his eyes. "Seems he sees the acquisition as some sort of experiment. If it works, fine, if not, Gerard's back in the swing of things in New York, and so nothing's lost."

"Nothing's lost?" Incredulous, Reginald jumped to his feet, pacing back and forth in front of the bench. This was madness. Everything he planned and sacrificed, including being saddled to a woman he didn't much like, let alone love, lost before it had even begun—all for the sake of money. The idea galled. "How much capital does this man have?"

Declan shook his head and leaned back against the rest. He positioned an elbow along the back. "That's not our biggest issue right now—"

"The hell it's not. And what do you mean, that's not our biggest issue?" Reginald stopped in front of his father and leaned forward. His words rose with the whistle of the wind. "Of course, it is…"

"No, actually, it's not." Declan draped a leg over the other.

Declan's casual pose belied the rage Reginald knew flared beneath. This was his father's business facade. The coil before the strike.

With measured tones, Declan continued. "In a fury, Peter called Mellon today and invited him to San Diego for the weekend. He's intent on the expansion now and wants Catherine to meet Arthur."

Chapter Nine

Within the span of a few days, the world as he knew it had imploded. For years he had orchestrated his life according to a pre-defined plan and now he was aimless. What had he been thinking? How had he allowed himself to be so bewitched? All of this sacrifice for a woman he barely knew.

After his father's revelation, Reginald had tried to speak to Peter but the man slammed the door in his face. From there, he'd invited Catherine for a drink before dinner, but as soon the music had started and Elleah took the stage, Catherine's face had hardened. In a determined fashion, with a stare colder than usual and her lips thinned, she rose from her seat and had fled the room, leaving Reginald in no doubt of the outcome between them.

As was the case earlier in the day, Reginald knew he should have chased after Catherine and not let her leave the lounge. She was his last hope of ever securing their place in the west. He understood that now. With their competitor so close on their heels, there was no longer any room for other options.

Despair raked him like nails; at the very least, he owed Catherine an explanation. For sure, he should find her and pleaded for a second chance. But he didn't. Against all common sense, he remained seated in the leather chaise, drink in hand, in a secluded corner made for lovers. Yet, he was alone. Something within him seemed intent to compel him toward disaster.

He drained the glass and pondered the facts. Even if he had followed Catherine, begged, cajoled, what could he say, in all honesty? He didn't *really* want her in his life. Deep down, he felt sure she knew that as well.

And with those glum realities circling his head, he lifted his hand to a passing waiter and ordered another drink. Vision foggy, thoughts swimming, back in his corner, he was as content as a leper left to his own scabs on a deliberately deserted island.

For the first time in his life, instead of anticipating a promising future, a particularly favored pastime these last few years, he abandoned habit and his usual Scotch. He ordered a tall whiskey, neat, and contemplated the curves of the luscious Miss Jaundoo. Where he should have been scheming—plotting his way back into favor with Peter and his daughter, Reginald leaned an elbow on the table and flagged down a refill. Tossing back the fiery liquid, he allowed the notes of her song to wash over him and imagined trailing his fingers along the exposed skin of her neckline, tracing the curve of her collarbone, and following this action with his lips before slowly relieving her of the garment.

How different she looked from the woman on the boardwalk, from the girl he'd helped on the beach. He shook his head and snickered. The sound rattled up his throat. He glanced around wondering who had released such a chortle. A chameleon, she shifted shape in different circumstances from innocence, to socialite, to seductress. With a woman like that at his side, Reginald was sure he could have anything he wanted. Very little would stand in his way with a partner like Elleah.

Yet she had, in fact, done nothing to seduce him. A shame really. Was that the reason for his compelling attraction? This annoying obsession he had developed over the last few days? Did he yearn for something not easily gained? Had life become too easy, too predictable, these last years?

With a sharp crack, he slapped a palm on the table and garnered the whispered stares of neighboring table occupants. He flapped fingers in their direction, telling them to mind their own business. What about the plot of this whole scheme—his plan—be the first to conquer both coasts and do something the other wealthy banking families hadn't yet done? "Boom," he said out loud and smirked at the startled faces that turned to stare at his sound effects. But it was true; all his plans had exploded.

One of the men from the table to his left flagged the waiter. Reginald watched from under hooded lids and kneaded the textured side of the glass. The etched crystal massaged the tips of his fingers. Reginald chuckled deep in his throat. What next?

The men glanced over and the waiter nodded.

He ignored them. Well, if he had achieved nothing else on this trip, he had at least come to some clarity—perspective, perhaps. Yes, he wanted to be successful in the business. Move through the second half of the millennium with fresh sails festooned for this new and savvy banker—their customer. He yearned to take the bank to the next level, but not at the sacrifice of his own personal happiness.

Would someone like Elleah make him happy? He returned his focus to the dais and watched her move across the stage. She had the ability to entrance the audience with both voice and dance.

The bugger of the reality was he didn't actually know what his personal happiness looked like. With each drink, he imagined an epiphany, or lucidity—some realization for direction, a course to weather the storm he had created. Like the haze from the cigars hovering around the ceiling fan, insight evaded his touch as much as the woman on the stage. Instead, all he might gain from his contemplations would likely be a hangover, while he enjoyed the sway of her hips and dreamed about what life would be like with her in his bed.

When Elleah sang, her smoky voice cloaked him in a warm embrace, and he all but felt her lips glide along his. His imagination included the tip of her tongue piercing his lips and, with this thought, his loins tightened. Her large eyes sought him out in the crowd, and she sang just for him.

Her form became hazy, and not from the growing cloud of smoke from the patrons. His teeth numbed and he dropped his glass more than once. The liquid pooled to the middle of the table. He stood, staggered, and righted himself to salute her, applauding loudly, causing a man from the bar to approach with a determined step.

"This is a dignified area, sir," said the stout Mexican with greased hair. The smell of his cologne permeated his senses, making his stomach roll. "Miss Jaundoo is a professional. You must settle yourself—"

"Y-yes, she certainly is," Reginald slurred. "I'll settle with another drink." He raised his empty glass.

The waiter laid a hand on Reginald's forearm. "I think we can finalize your bill, Mr. Cavanaugh, and call it an evening."

Reginald shook off the hold. The lights suddenly seemed too bright and the attention from the other patrons made him feel their conspiracy against him. "Bloody hell, we will." He pushed back from the small table and his chair crashed to the floor.

The music stopped, and a general gasp hung with the smoke rings. The eruption of whispers replaced the music.

Was he now the show? "Sing," he called above the crowd to the Elleah who gazed back, silent, microphone in hand.

Sweat broke out above his lip and swiped the back of his hand across his face. He had to escape. Everywhere he turned, rejection followed. Reginald waved a hand expansively across the crowd, took a bow in mock gratification for their attention, and staggered toward the exit. He flung off an offered hand of assistance and banged into a wall.

"Mr. Cavanaugh, sir. Allow me to see you to your room."

Reginald couldn't hold the man in focus and shook his head. "I'm f-fine." He tugged his shirt in place and pitched through the exit door.

Out in the fresh air, Reginald heard the music resume within moments. Elleah's throaty voice spoke to the crowd, drawing their attention.

"Goddamnit." He raked his fingers through his hair. *She was supposed to only sing for me.*

He lurched toward the beckoning sound of the ocean. A chill caught him, and he realized he'd forgotten his jacket back in the lounge. He waved a contemptuous hand. What did he care?

On the sand, he staggered, fell to one knee, took a breath to regulate his balance, and resumed his trek. Within a few more steps, he located a beach chair close at hand. Pausing to take aim, he flung himself across the cushions. He landed close enough and remained enmeshed in his own torment while the effects of the booze swam through his veins.

The mist soaked his shirt, but Reginald didn't bother to move. Where would he go? Everything he had worked for these last years, everything he had planned, was gone—washed away like the rivulets of water he watched course down the arm of the beach chair.

A cold shiver coursed through him, raising gooseflesh along his arms, but he hadn't the energy to care. With a valiant heave, he rolled onto his back and extended his hands to cover his face. He groaned and pressed his palms against his lids, wishing, like a child, the move could erase his actions of the past week. If he could turn back time… No, it didn't matter, nothing would change. He wouldn't risk not meeting Elleah. Even at a moment where all seemed lost.

Instead, he strove to dislodge the original plan and his lack of preparedness to see it through to the end.

He flung the moisture back from his cheeks and stared up into the clearing night. The mist lessened and heaven's offered an endless black sky. The blue-black space was dispersed with an occasional murky-colored cloud, and he felt as vacant as the emptiness of the universe. What was out there anyway? Nothing. The same as what sat within him, what opportunity await his future. Nothing.

There, feeling as small as a grain of sand, Reginald tried to see through the galaxy to what may await him.

Lost in time and space, he didn't know how long he had been in one place. But after a while, the world began to spin and he lurched to the side, fighting sickness. With a hand wrapped around the armrest, held onto the side of the chaise to retain his balance.

"My grandfather always suggested putting your foot on the ground," a soft voice commanded. "Contact with the Earth tricks the mind into stopping the spinning sensation. It'll keep you from vomiting."

****

As a man who stood out from the crowd, Reginald wasn't hard to find. After knocking softly on his door to see if he had made it back to his room, Elleah didn't stop to question her all-consuming need to find him. She simply changed into more serviceable clothes, threw on her best walking shoes and a cardigan. Glancing out her window to see the drops of water on the pane, she grabbed up the shawl draped over her chair and wrapped it across her shoulders. Then, with as quick a motion as her healed ankle would allow, she made her way to the beach boardwalk. Because of her previous encounter with him on the beach, she was drawn in that general direction. He wouldn't be far, she surmised. As inebriated as he had seemed, and despite the time lag, she couldn't imagine he had walked a great distance on his own steam.

She rubbed her palms together as she walked. Pausing under the lamp, she lifted her wrist to check the time display on the slender gold watch. Less than an hour since his outburst. She shook her head and looked to the sky, glad the rain had stopped.

A voice, strongly resembling her father's, echoed in her mind that she should let the likes of Reginald

Cavanaugh go and be done with it. But a longing to comfort propelled her forward. She had witnessed such pain this evening and couldn't deny the attraction.

Did the man have no one who cared? So pitiful was his profile in the bar, she couldn't keep her heart from breaking. He appeared so forlorn and lost, completely abandoned by all who had, only that afternoon, surrounded him with gaiety and laughter. What kind of people turned on one of their own so quickly?

She knew the answer to the question all too well. The same people she refused to allow to embrace, or reject, her at their will.

Obviously things had not been straightened out between him and his fiancée—or no, not his fiancée—Elleah's heart leaped at the prospect that he was not married, nor engaged. She chose to ignore the common sense side of her brain, which outlined the folly of her actions. Devil be damned, she would no longer deny her fascination. Perhaps the time had come for her to stop running from her fears and face them head on.

Her feet sank in the wet sand. The heaviness of the moisture-laden granules lodged in the seams of her sandals and slowed her progress. Scared to re-injure her bad ankle, she bent to remove her shoes. She'd be better off walking barefoot rather than taking shovelfuls of sand with each step. Standing, she could just make out a large shadow sprawled on the first row of empty loungers. Instinctively, she recognized the tall form as Reginald.

With caution, Elleah approached slowly, uncertain of her next move. As she came closer, even in the dim light, she could see the shivers of cold vibrating along his flesh. She removed the shawl she had wrapped over her sweater and draped it around his shoulders.

He moaned.

She assumed, something of gratitude. "You're welcome."

He struggled to sit up, hand reaching into the air, only to fall back down. "Wh-why?" He cleared his throat.

She wished she had thought to bring water.

"Why are you here?"

Giving a groan and a grunt of exertion, she dragged a nearby lounger close to his across the damp sand. Wiping her brow, she sat on the edge, aware of the puddle in the middle. She leaned to examine him, coming up short with a reasonable explanation, unwilling to delve into her urges when it came to Reginald. Finally, she shook her head. "I don't really know."

He chuckled. "C-come—" he hiccupped loudly, with an audible intake of air. "To take advantage of me?"

She swept a hand across his cheek, tracing a line down to his biceps, and then tucked the shawl around his shoulders. Her lips quirked. "Perhaps."

He opened one eye. "I'm all yours." He rolled his head on the cushion to the sound of the ocean, then back to her and closed the one eye as though it was too heavy for the effort.

Her stomach clenched. Really? She had little experience with drunk men, but based on Reginald's current state, would consider them highly unreliable despite the quickening of pulse with his words. She curled her toes in the sand, dropping her shoes on the edge of the chaise. "Are you, now?" She brushed the stubborn forelock aside from his brow. "And why is that?"

He had either fallen asleep or was taking an inordinate amount of time to ponder the question. Elleah resisted the inclination to settle back in her chair with the puddle just waiting for her bottom. Instead, she waited, unsure what to do next. She reached to touch him again, but instead folded her arms across her chest and straightened her spine. Regardless of circumstances with his lady, Catherine, he remained the forbidden fruit.

But she was tempted. By God, she was. Eyes adjusted to the dim light, Elleah gazed upon his serene face. He looked younger than usual. This did little to alleviate the attraction. Vulnerability etched the downward turn of his closed lids and the thinness of his pouting mouth.

Obviously, she couldn't move him on her own. And even if she could, would she want to and take a chance on being seen? Perhaps he didn't care about his reputation, but she certainly did. The last thing she needed was any of the hotel staff seeing her with a man, most especially the same man who'd made a scene this evening.

"You f-fac-cin-ate-nate me," Reginald responded at last.

Elleah started and inadvertently sat back in the water accumulated on her chair. "Ohhh." Having taken so long, she thought he had fallen asleep. With a fruitless swipe across her bum, she shifted forward to lean toward him, hovering inches above his face. "Is that why you propositioned me?"

He shook his head. "Don't know what I was

thinking?"

"You made it pretty clear what you were thinking."

His boyish smile connected with deep dimples and revealed a slight cleft in his chin. "Just another in a long line of mistakes."

"Shush," she soothed, and gave in to temptation. Moved by his sincerity, she stroked his cheek. The tips of her fingers scratched across the stubble. "Surely nothing is lost that you cannot fix."

He shrugged his shoulders. An awkward movement given his position. "There's where you are wrong," he said, before proceeding to outline his plan conceived in New York to be implemented in California.

His voice gained strength in the telling, and she heard the steel of resolve. That he was prepared to go to such lengths to get what he wanted shocked her. Then to find out he was of the Cavanaugh family, long-time rivals of the Mellons, wasn't as much a surprise as she may have once thought. To say she was familiar with the name was an understatement. Intense rivalry had existed for at least a generation between the senior Cavanaugh and her father. Resigned to her own damp garment, she crossed her ankles and considered him, glad of her own alias. The last thing she wanted to give him was an excuse to seduce her for her portion of the Mellon empire.

Elleah pulled the cardigan closer and shook her head. Somehow, she had known Reginald was a businessman from New York. In her gut, she had a feeling they may have even ran in the same social circles but had never connected.

To have his profession nailed down to banking was merely to put a finer point on the issue. His plan, however, now revealed, showed her how shrewdly calculating he was at heart. Truly, watching him relate the intrigues of his boldness, his face so full of regret, made it hard to connect this man to the conductor of a plan who could deal with people—his family—a future wife—without any kind empathy. Could this man, with his hands pressed against his cheeks in regret, be so coldly calculating? She breathed deeply, the salty air filling her lungs lifted a burden. In her heart, she couldn't accept it.

"Then there's Mellon," Reginald continued, lowering his hands from his face, his voice growing stronger.

Elleah pulled back from her slouch and sat tall. She bent her knees to the side, crossed her ankles, and laced her fingers in her lap. "Another banker?" She kept her voice soft and cautious. What would he say about her father—or was it her brother he referenced?

Reginald lifted his arms, only to let them flop to his sides. "We were never ahead of him after all."

"No?" She sat unmoving, listening.

"No." Reginald rolled to his side and dropped his fingers to the sand. "He's already here."

"Here?" Elleah looked over her shoulder, searching her surroundings, expecting her brother to walk across the beach. Had Arthur not returned home? Was her father now in California too? Were they here at the Del? Her stomach tightened and her heart lodged in her throat.

"He's purchased a building in LA. And Peter, curse his black heart, invited the young buck here to put Catherine in his path." Reginald paused then shook his head. "He's no better than a whoremaster strutting his

97

wares before potential buyers."

The irony wasn't lost on Elleah. She relaxed at the prospect of Arthur's return to the Del, instead of her father's. She had little to say to her father after a very vocal rejection of Bryan, his main prospect for her to marry "because it would be good for business." But her brother—she had handled him once and felt secure she could do it again.

She bit her lip and contemplated her next move. Should she stay or go? Arthur and Catherine? An unlikely pairing. But, what did she know of these things? Her brain raced ahead, planning and weighing the circumstances either way.

"My fault, really," Reginald continued. He built a small castle from the damp sand. "If it weren't for me, Peter wouldn't have ever set his sights on California, and certainly Catherine wouldn't be the object of purchase to entice him here." Fisting his hand, he smashed the castle, leaving a dent in its wake.

Elleah couldn't dally further. Rising from her seat and assuming he was sober enough to walk, she coaxed Reginald to his feet to motivate him back to his room. Keeping to the shadows, she pushed him on his way once she reached the stairwell, telling him she had a quick errand to attend to before returning to her own room.

In fact, she slipped around the building to another entrance and made her way slowly back to her room to avoid running into, or being seen with, Reginald.

She approached the room with a slow pace over the carpet. As she passed Reginald's room, she noticed he had left the door unlocked. She paused and glanced across the hall to her own suite. Just a quick look to ensure he's okay. Once she verified he was safe in his bed, she would seek the welcoming comfort of her own. *And that would be that.* She rubbed her hands together as though to rid herself of dust, ending with palms out to show finality.

By the time Elleah returned to her own suite, shortly before the sun poked its head above the horizon, she had made up her mind. Tonight would be her last show at the Del. She had to get as far away from Reginald, his temptation, and the potential of being found out as she could.

****

The sun cut a swath through his room, razoring shards of light beneath his lids, forcing him to wake. With heavy limbs, Reginald rolled out of the path of light, his brain sloshing in his skull like liquid swish in barrel, altering balance with each movement. Summoning his courage with a deep breath, Reginald sat up in bed. His hands shot to brace his head, leveraging the weight.

Moaning, he opened his eyes. On his bedside table sat a glass of water and two tablets. Grateful to whatever angel laid the restorative at his fingertips, he downed the pills with the water in one gulp. Anticipating the curative powers swirling through the booze in his bloodstream, he took stock of his surroundings. He couldn't remember returning to his room last night. In fact, he couldn't recall much of anything after leaving the lounge. Or could he.

Images flashed like a slide show without context. Reginald searched his sketchy memory…singing…mist…Elleah…lips…warmth…unfamiliar sensations. Was it just a dream? Damn it, he couldn't nail anything down. His recollection was like looking through a fishbowl.

He turned to set the glass back on the stand when his gaze fastened on his tie. The red Hermes tie he had used to bind Elleah's ankle. There it lay—clean, neatly pressed, and folded.

She *had* been with him last night. It wasn't his imagination. He glanced to the other side of the bed, hopeful. Not even a dent marked the other pillow. He ran a hand across his bare chest and looked down at his boxer shorts. Had he undressed himself? How he wished he could remember. He glanced to the carpet willing his mind to work. Sandy footprints trailed across the pattern—two sets.

A smile curved his lips in anticipation of asking her when he *happened* to see her again—soon.

Chapter Ten

Elleah heaved the larger of the patterned suitcases off the bed and set it next to the others. She had finished packing. Except for her overnighter with the essentials, her bags lay neatly stacked by the armoire, ready for departure in the morning. Henry, the entertainment manager, wasn't pleased at all when she informed him she had accepted another gig elsewhere. He was one of the few she wouldn't miss.

He ranted and raved, but in the end, what could he do? The diminutive manager proved to be a master of the cold shoulder. Henry provided her with the silent treatment all through rehearsal.

Little did he know, he made her decision easier— less remorse. Elleah considered his lack of attention a blessing.

Jacques rushed over when she passed the dining room on the way back to her suite.

"Do tell me it's not true, moi Cheri," Jacques said with a pout in his phony accent. "It's all over the kitchens. The staff are heartbroken you are leaving. Henry is in an absolute tizzy, and management said he should have treated you better. For such talent to just walk away…"

Elleah tilted her head to the side and patted his arm. "You are too kind, Jacques, and I shall miss you."

"You will come back." He laid tentative fingers on

top of her hand.

Elleah glanced at his touch, then back into his chocolate gaze. "Perhaps." If only someone like Jacques could make her happy. She knew he was willing, but Jacques, with his fake brogue, which still boasted a Mexican trill, wasn't for her.

Butterflies flitted in her stomach as she dressed for the show. She selected a golden gown, fitted to hug her curves and accentuate the lines of her figure to their best advantage. The neckline stretched across her collarbone from shoulder cap to shoulder cap. The back fell in a soft fold to her tailbone. Designed to titillate the observer, the dress covered and revealed all at the same time. From her hips, the filmy fabric dropped to a puddle around her feet. The thigh-high slit opened and closed as she walked, adding to its allure.

The gown was one her mother had commissioned for her coming out, which never did happen. Elleah lifted a forefinger to run under her eye. Society no longer had meaning. Or, better put, the meaning it represented was no longer positive. And now, with the entrance of Reginald into her life, he only served to reinforce her belief that she had no place within the current structure of New York aristocracy.

Elleah shook her head at her reflection, missed her mark with the liner, and left a black streak on her eyelid. "Oh, bother." She corrected her makeup, assessed the result, and put her pencils away. With her elbow on the dressing table, she sat with her chin on the cuff of her hand, staring without seeing. "What will I do now?"

She had no idea where she would go next. All she knew was she had to leave the Del behind. This lovely old hotel had sheltered her these last months when she needed mending, allowing her the time come into herself, her own independence. But now the time had arrived to say goodbye. Reginald could never know who she was—that she was an heiress to a great fortune accumulated through his rival. Elleah placed a gloved hand on her abdomen and sucked in a deep breath. Despite her feelings, she wouldn't become his next 'mark' to further his ambitions.

These strong emotions she had quickly developed for him would have to be forgotten just as rapidly. "Keep moving forward," she said with a definitive nod, stood, and strode toward the door.

****

His father's presence made Reginald second-guess his decisions. Declan had this impact on most people.

Trailing his fingers along the soft sheets, back and forth, he had pondered the untouched pillow on his bed a long time. Neither a dent nor even a stray hair gave evidence she was ever in his room. Yet, he could feel the smoothness of her skin under his palm. He rubbed his thumb and forefinger together. He could swear he remembered the texture of her lustrous locks between his fingertips. His body tightened in expectation, he wanted her there, right now. And how. The more he contemplated his situation, the more he longed for her—the lady with the golden skin—the songbird—the feisty cat. Yes, he wanted it all—the full package, no holding back. Elleah was a woman he could wake up with in the morning. A woman he could talk to, spar with, engage on an intellectual level. He liked that about her personality. She was lively and had startled him out from whatever trance he had been under. Now that he was awake, he never wanted to sleep again.

After a much needed cold shower, Reginald dressed with decision. He was done with the pretense, the scheming, and the constant calculation of the chess game of business. Meeting Elleah had finally put things in perspective.

He literally skipped down the stairwell to the dining room. Casting his gaze across the assembled diners, he didn't spot his father in their usual table by the window. Undeterred, he ordered the breakfast of champions—eggs, bacon, hash browns, and toast—before leaving his cozy corner in search of Declan.

Giving the doorman a wave, he proceeded through the glass doors toward the gardens off the back courtyard, not far from the surfside restaurant.

"You are looking quite fresh for a fellow who has upended everything we planned," Declan began without preamble, dragging deeply of his cigarette. He paced to and fro in front of the roses, sure not to benefit from the excess of tar in the otherwise fresh morning air.

Reginald strolled to the bench, sat, and draped an arm over the back. "I don't think so," he said with a smile, using his free hand to adjust the pleat in his freshly laundered pants.

"How's that?" Declan walked through the cloud of smoke toward Reginald. His eyes squinted against the draw of the burn, drawing deep lines down the contours of his face. "You've a new plan?"

"Not completely." Reginald crossed his legs. He rested his palm upon his knee. "More like the beginnings of an idea. Something workable."

"Well, don't keep me waiting." Declan strode to sit next to Reginald, flicking ash off the end of the fag.

"Out with it."

Reginald focused on Declan's face. "We go it alone. Cut Peter loose. He's a—"

Declan jumped to his feet, flicking the cigarette stub into the bushes and raising his arms heavenward. "And have him join Mellon? Have you lost your senses?"

"Not at all," Reginald returned, keeping his tones smooth, covering the anxiety eating like acid up his esophagus. "We may not have the chain right away, but we have enough to make a start and hold our own. I've been looking into this. Credit cards are the way of the future. We broached this subject last year, but found it too much of a risk. After all we've done this year to prepare, the risk is negligible at best. Think of it—lines of credit for the common Joe."

Declan faced him, hands on his hips, his breath coming in short gasps. His stare seemed to burn a hole through Reginald. A move Reginald knew was meant to unnerve him. A vein throbbed in the skeletal temple and his mouth moved without vocals. Finally, the older man reached inside his pocket, pulled out a fresh cigarette and lit it using his engraved golden lighter. "Is Catherine really so bad?" His voice was a hoarse whisper.

His father sounded genuinely concerned. The tone was so foreign Reginald lost his train of thought. "Pardon?"

His brow pinched over his nose. "Son, I know it's not a love match, but you never struck me as the sentimental type."

Reginald threw his head back and laughed. Of all the people in the world, his father was the last person he would have expected to have such a conversation. Despite the caring tendencies of the exchange, Reginald would not reveal his underbelly, not even to his father. He had learned young how his father twisted and manipulated any perceived weakness.

Reginald stood and slapped his father on the shoulder, getting back to business. "Not sentimental...practical. Let's face it, I—no correct that—*we*—the bank's future—needs a match with a bit more spark. Catherine's a wallflower." He held up a hand to stall his father's response. "I know who she is and about her breeding, but we've bigger plans than the Burrs could ever support, and I need a progressive partner—"

His father coughed. "You're not considering the entertainer?"

Reginald turned back around to the bench and resumed his seat.

"No, no, my boy. Surely not." Declan sat and slapped a hand on Reginald's knee before crossing his legs and leaning back. "Absolutely not. We will be going political, and that means scrutiny." Declan threw his arms in the air. "Remove her from any plan you may have concocted." Then he stood and strode back toward the hotel.

Reginald sat forward on the bench, dropped his elbows to his knees, and let his head hang. His father hadn't even considered his concept of being on the ground floor of the newest development called "credit cards". He pulled a deep lungful of air in through his nose. His lungs hurt and his heart raced as though he had run a marathon and had forgotten to breathe. Had he given his future away and gained nothing to look forward to?

He stamped his foot and stood to glare across the expanse of garden. Hell or high water, he would get what he wanted. He marched with purpose the length of the lawns, through the double glass doors and across lobby of the hotel.

****

With so much to do, the day had passed in a blur. At last, her final show. She touched her fingers to her stomach to quell the bittersweet butterflies. Finally, the lights dimmed and the music started. Gaining her mark, Elleah stepped up on the stage and glided toward the microphone. Though the crowd lay in shadows, she felt their gaze upon her. She nodded at the conductor, closed her eyes, pictured the notes floating behind her lids, felt the pull of the chords, drew her breath, and released her song.

She scanned the crowd. Dancers had taken to the floor, their bodies flowing to the harmony. Elleah smiled to encourage participation. Her hand held close to her breast, extended forward to emphasize the words of the song. Then she turned her palm skyward and followed the mark at the end of her fingers like a marksman sighting his prey. And there, at the back of the room, shoulder against the wall, arms folded across his chest stood Reginald as though summoned. A quirk of his lips nudged his cheeks. Unable to resist, she grinned back. She couldn't help it. He drew her, and because she couldn't resist the attraction, she had to go.

Concentrating to not lose her placement in the harmony, Elleah broke eye contact and forced her gaze to travel around the room. The doctor and his wife had returned. A few other regulars waved in acknowledgement of her attention. As she sang, she nodded back.

One set of lyrics led into another and yet, Reginald held his place. He clapped when everyone else clapped, acknowledged the service staff, and held his drink without actually draining the contents. Every once in a while, despite aching to look elsewhere, she'd watch him swirl the liquor, the amber liquid would catch the light.

He was focused and intense. Even from this distance, Elleah could sense the tension coming off him in waves. He was coiled tight and ready to spring. He was the hunter, and she knew, the current of attraction arching between them, she was his prey.

And just like the hunter, he waited in the shadows for his moment.

The quiver in her stomach reflected anticipation rather than fear. She should be planning to leave, instead of the sudden contemplation on how to stay. The hairs on her arms stood tall, craving his touch. She knew, beyond a doubt, should she be given an opportunity, she didn't have the will to resist his pull. Elleah wanted him as badly as she envisioned he wanted her. For that reason, if for no other, she had to leave, else she would surely compromise herself.

Silence hushed in on the room and she bent to take a sip of her now cool tea. The conductor glanced over his shoulder to her and winked. She nodded. Just one more set and then she would be free. The employee stairwell to the back of the stage would allow her to escape without going through the crowd. Perhaps she would leave tonight, instead of in the morning, as planned.

So torn between her thoughts, she almost missed her next cue and started the song on the second stanza.

The conductor turned to face her, his smile gone and gave her a warning glare.

She smiled sweetly and shrugged her shoulders. Tomorrow would be fine. Surely she could avoid Reginald just one more night. She ended the internal conflict with decision.

Finished, Elleah bowed to the applause and started descending the stairs, waving at the good doctor, when she sighted Reginald approaching. Placing her palms flat to her stomach, she drew herself tall, grateful she was back in her heels. They gave her some height, marginal though it may be.

A grin lit his face. "You really love to sing," he began, stepping close, yet maintaining a safe distance. He swept his arms, then folded them across his chest. "I especially liked the last one."

"Thank you," she replied simply, aching to flee, yet her pride held her still. Nerves danced along her skin and her pulse raced loud in her ears. She had to focus to hear him. Leaning forward, she watched his lips move, imagining kissing them, rather than listening to the sounds being produced.

"I wanted to thank you for last evening," he said.

Finding a spot for his feet he held his ground, dropping his arms, palm upward to his sides. His jaw worked and he tilted his head. It was a boyish move and Elleah caught her breath. The gesture reinforced his abundance of charm.

"I was an ass and you helped me anyway."

She tore her gaze from his lips and strove to center her attention on his eyes. A dancing light of mischief lit their depths, making her know he understood very well his impact on her. She licked her lips, mentally dousing the fire in her belly. "Well…we all have our moments."

"Not you."

She shook her head. "Everyone."

He reached for her hand.

Elleah allowed him to sweep her fingers into his grasp.

He covered her fingers with his palm and held them encapsulated in their warmth. "There's something about you."

Her heart quickened. Even the back of her knees tingled as she imagined the lightness of his gentle fingers tracing their way along her body. The sounds of the crowd muted, and even the stage lighting seemed to fade, leaving only she and Reginald in the room.

"You've intrigued me from the beginning…without a doubt. But you're more than that. You have a quality." His thumb traced a pattern across the tops of her fingers. "You may say we don't know each other, but I feel like we do. From the beginning, you're uncompromising. There's no pretense. Like a light in a storm, you draw me. No matter how I've tried, I can't get you out of my mind, Elleah. I want to…" He lifted her fingers to his lips and kissed the tips gently. "Won't you let me know you better?"

How she wished she were, in fact, what she seemed, but the truth would come out one way or another, and then what? To give herself to this man would be easy. But he wasn't this man. He was a ruthless capitalist, willing to go to any lengths to get what he wanted. For now, she offered a distraction. Yes, if he knew who she really was, then she had no doubt he would pursue her. But if she remained Elleah the singer, would his affection be genuine for the long term?

So many questions and doubts swirled. She bit her lip, striving to get hold of her rampant, rebellious emotions. With a slight tug, she pulled her hand from his grasp. Praying her voice would stay strong and not belie the impact of his touch and words. "I'm single. I'm different from the…ah…ladies you are used to accompanying." Elleah lifted her chin and moved her eyes to the upper landings of the hotel. "That's the intrigue I hold. Every soon-to-be married man feels the tug and draw of the chain. You are questioning your freedom." Before she revealed how much she knew, Elleah stopped the flow of words. Searching his eyes, she could see none of the callous, cold-blooded planner he divulged the night before. Standing in front of her now was a man with a woman, and she had to remind herself of the trap. She had to steer clear.

He matched his palms together and folded the fingers. Bending his head, he rubbed the fingers under his chin. "I'm not engaged, Elleah."

She stepped back. "Not yet."

He took a marginal step forward and dropped his arms. His eyes grew large. "Not ever, to Catherine or anyone else. Never close, never wanted to be close, as you say to the chain—until now."

Elleah's heart skipped, and she banked down her hope. Could she really believe him? She firmed her spine and forced a smile to keep her resolve. "Has anyone told Catherine?"

"Oh, I think Catherine will be just fine." Reginald clasped his hands behind his back. "Her father is introducing her to the young Mr. Mellon this evening. Peter is hoping for—"

"Tonight? Arthur?" The questions escaped before she could reel them in. With a half turn, she glanced around the crowd, searching for her brother. She had hoped to be gone before his arrival. Had she cut her departure too close?

Reginald reached for her arm. "You know him? How?"

She glanced quickly at Reginald before turning toward the stage entrance, yanking out of his grasp. "I have to go." She started to stride away.

"Wait." Reginald followed close behind. "What's wrong?"

Elleah flapped her hands and shook her head. Suddenly the room echoed with resounding noise and the lights intensified their brightness. Her ears perked, expecting Arthur at any moment. She couldn't allow him to see her with Reginald. He would surely interfere with her flight plans. She lifted her skirts and increased her pace to the back of the stage.

Reginald regained his hold on her upper arm and stepped up to her side. "I don't understand. Is this Arthur a threat to you? I can help."

She had no doubt he would. "No," Elleah said, looking this way and that unable to determine the best route and how to get rid of Reginald. "You are of no help to me at all. I must go."

"But, I don't want you to go. I want—"

She stopped searching the crowd and faced him. "You want only to get into my bed." Her words slashed through the air, and his stunned expression made her know she had hit her mark. She glared and wrenched free her arm. "Now, let me go."

"You heard my daughter," a deep voice interjected. "Unhand her, now."

Chapter Eleven

An electrical shock wouldn't have jolted him so badly. Reginald dropped his hold on Elleah's arm and stepped back a pace. "Mellon!" The word shot out of his mouth like a bullet in a silent room. The surname of his family's archrival, the bane of his present predicament, struck him with equal impact. Recognition of the man standing to his right, scowling at him, face pinched in fury, fueled the flame. What could Gerard Mellon possibly want with Elleah? Had he heard the man correctly—daughter?

"Daddy!" Elleah's voice sounded both troubled and scared. She did not step toward him or offer any form of affection. Her eyes were wide and she bit her lip, leaving an imprint. "What are you doing here?"

"Daddy?" Reginald lifted the cuff of his hand to his forehead and pushed across his brow line, stunned with revelation. But her name was Jaundoo. He flashed his gaze between the two. Jaundoo or Mellon, there was no denying the obvious resemblance in the shape of their faces and eye color. With effort, he schooled his face into a mask of neutrality. He dropped his hand to swipe a non-existent speck from his suit jacket, vying for time to calm his racing thoughts. At last he faced Elleah and drawled, "You're a Mellon?"

Mellon's eyes narrowed. "And who, sir, are you?" The words were clipped. His faded Americanized

British accent rang like a hallmark over the "sir". "And what business have you with my daughter?"

Gerard Mellon was a man built to adapt perfectly into his attire, his six-foot frame being neither too tall, nor too short. The older man gave off an aura of superiority without ostentatiousness. Mellon was healthy for his age, sporting no noticeable belly. Given his widowed state, and the grief people proclaimed had wracked, and nearly ruined his business, Reginald was surprised. Equally extraordinary was a man of his stature and good looks, never mind enviable fortune, remained single these two years since his wife's death.

Not to be outdone, Reginald drew himself tall, needing the extra inches he had over this imposing man. "Reginald Cavanaugh," he replied and held out his hand to shake. He'd be damned if he would be cowed by Mellon. He'd done nothing to deserve the hostility.

Mellon eyed the outstretched appendage for a second longer than socially acceptable before grasping his palm in a firm squeeze. "A Cavanaugh, is it? You're here with Peter Burr and company?"

Reginald squared his shoulders. Combat and accusation colored the man's every syllable. "Yes, the Burrs accompanied *us* on this trip."

Mellon released his grip and lodged a thumb in his trouser pocket. His fingers tapped staccato on his hip, accentuating the pause. "Interesting." He nodded.

Reginald had the impression he'd been dismissed. But explanations were in order. As he pivoted to face Mellon, the older man turned to address his daughter.

"Ell—"

"What is?" Reginald broke in, forcing Mellon's attention.

"Excuse me?" Mellon tilted his head partially back to gaze at Reginald. He raised a brow while his eyes narrowed their focus.

Reginald knew he should leave off with any conversation. Heat had begun to creep up his neck. Whatever was between father and daughter didn't include him, despite his curiosity. But Elleah mattered to him, and something about the man's arrogance grated. Not bothering to face Reginald man to man, Mellon had dismissed Reginald as though he were a small boy who required a reprimand from his parents. "What is interesting to you?"

Mellon faced Reginald squarely and took his measure from head-to-toe. "I like the cut of your suit, Cavanaugh."

"Thank you—"

"But I do not like the cut of your business practices." Mellon crossed his arms over his chest, while his fingers continued their patter on his immaculate jacket sleeves. "I was invited here by Peter. We have been acquaintances for years. He especially wanted Arthur to become reacquainted with their daughter, Catherine. But now that I know the Burrs are only here due to the behest of a Cavanaugh leads me to view this meeting with different eyes."

The man's lack of regard for social nuance, cutting straight to the point, smarted. Reginald resisted the urge to step back. Considering they had only met a few times prior to this, his open hostility cut through his casual mask. Before tonight, Reginald had never given Mellon an opportunity to dislike him. This instant animosity disarmed him. "What is your meaning?" he asked, slipping a hand in his pocket to maintain an air of calm.

Mellon sighed and raised a hand to his chin. "Excuse me one moment, my dear," he said over his shoulder to Elleah. Turning back to Reginald, he crossed his arms again. "In the early days, many of our customers were one-time Cavanaugh bankers who lost their investments—their savings, leaving them to flounder…"

"Everyone lost in the early days—"

"Not Cavanaugh," Mellon cut in. "Nor did you even try to assist. Instead, you took whatever profit—"

"That was before my time, *sir*," Reginald shot back, hot shame racing up his spine. He refused to defend practices he had no hand in. Instead, he took an offensive tactic. "And certainly not appropriate conversation for present company."

"Then you shouldn't have asked," Mellon snapped. He straightened his arms and adjusted the sleeves of his finely cut suit by the cuffs. "Further, that you are here only provides me with more motivation to move forward with Arthur's plans. The people of California should not be subjected to your kind of business, *sir*," he sneered. "And to think, I thought at first Arthur was mad with this idea."

Reginald took a breath to respond, but Mellon apparently wasn't finished.

"Whatever your dealings with my daughter, call them to an end. Right now. This is a private matter." He turned his back on Reginald, effectively cutting off any response.

Elleah gaped, glanced at Reginald, then back at Mellon as her father took her by her elbow and led her out of sight behind the stage area.

****

Elleah gasped. She was moving too fast for her sore ankle. She pulled against his grip and forced him to slow his stride.

"Daddy." Elleah found it hard to both breathe and think. She was tired of being manhandled by the opposite sex tonight. Who did they think she was to be led about without considering her wants or needs.

Once Gerard slowed his step, she wrenched her arm free from his firm grasp. "What are you doing? Let me go this instant. I haven't seen you in so long, and the first thing you do is cause a scene."

Her father's eyes rounded, but he dropped his hand.

She wanted to hug him and run from him all at the same time. But she was no longer his little girl who couldn't face her father's determined stance. Almost two years ago, she had left his house, heartbroken from the loss of her mother and rebellious that she wouldn't marry Bryan. She'd grown a lot since then. Her father wasn't all that different from the multitude of other men she had encountered.

His lips thinned as he paused to look around their surroundings. "At the moment…I'm contemplating the fastest route to remove you from this situation. How could you have allowed yourself to stoop to such a level—entertaining men in a lounge?"

His words smeared over the meaning, making them dirty and guttural. She reached a gloved hand to cover her nose and mouth and hung her head. Considering all she had achieved in her independence, never once dipping into her trust, securing a job, lodging and managing to take care of herself, Elleah stiffened her spine to stand straight and proud. Looking him square in the eye, she would not be made ashamed of her profession. She had done nothing to soil her reputation.

He looked so much older than she remembered. The gray, which used to only highlight his temples, had invaded to the point where he was more white than brown. Combed smartly as always, he couldn't hide the receding hairline, which made his prominent nose even more an object of notice. His arrogance of moments before lacked his old spark, and haggardness dragged at his eyes. However, there was no denying his disapproving frown.

"Not unlike Mama when you first met her," Elleah shot back, having rehearsed this scene many times in anticipation of being 'found' at some point.

He lifted his chin and glared at her from the advantage of his height. "Certainly not the same at all."

She would not be intimidated. "No?" She braced both hands on her hips to keep them from shaking.

"Certainly not! Unlike her, your mother made sure you had nothing but choice and opportunity, and..." His arm shot wide to encompass the surroundings. "You threw it all away—here—with them." He snorted and cross his arms. "Go gather your things. I'll take you back to New York." He fluttered his fingers off the crook of his sleeve to shoo her toward his prescribed chore. "Or, better yet, leave them. We'll buy new. A nice shopping trip will likely be a welcome change I'm sure."

The heat of a flush crept rapidly up her neck. Her fingers tingled where she resisted the urge to slap him for his assumptions. But stronger was the hot sting of tears that threatened. How dare he barge into her life and threaten to take over! She stood staring at him; this was not as she had imagined their reunion. She was unable to form words. This…bastard…was not the man of her childhood—the loving father.

"What would your mother think of all of this?" He made a point of casting his gaze wide to take in the dusty dank of the back room where she often waited to go on stage. "This isn't what she wanted for you."

Finally, her voice curled up from the depths of her diaphragm. "Don't march in on me after all of this time and presume to lecture me on what Mama would or wouldn't have wanted. I can tell you plenty of what she *wouldn't have wanted* for me when you became a tyrant after she died. Do you think she *would have wanted* me to marry Bryan simply because he was good for business?" She paused, gasping heavily. Then she pointed her finger to connect with his chest. "You bear no resemblance to the man I knew as my father growing up. What would Mama say about *you*?"

His face flushed scarlet then paled. A vein became visible along his neck. "How dare you." His nose flared.

He reached for her and grabbed her by her shoulders. "I miss her, too. I loved your mother like I could never love another." He shook just a bit.

Elleah tried to step back, but his grip was like an iron vise. Never one for violence, his bulging eyes scared her no less.

Then his eyes misted and he blinked several times. As she stared, she saw the anguish filling their depth. She had gone too far. "I know," she said, and looked down, ashamed at her words. "But you refused to see…Arthur and I missed her, too—"

He pulled her close and hugged her fiercely. "I

have looked for you since the day you left. Do you have any idea what it's been like?" Mellon straightened his arms, holding her at arms length. "From one end of this country to the other, I have hired people to find you." His voice shook, and his breathing was audible, the unshed tears bathed his eyes. "I should never have put you in such a position."

She lifted her chin. "I'm a grown woman, Daddy. I'll not marry whomever you choose. I have my own ideas and ambitions."

He shook his head. "I only want what's best for you—"

"You don't always *know* what's best—"

"Certainly, I know enough to say a *Cavanaugh* is not what's best. And certainly not the likes of that philanderer." He gave her shoulders another slight shake, his words strong again. "If he is anything remotely close to his reputation or his sire…"

"You don't know," she gasped, pulling back from his touch. "You don't know anything about him."

"And you do?" Her father dropped his hands by his sides. He stood tall and looked down the length of his nose, eyes cleared of all moisture. His gaze turned frosty while he searched her face. Accusation lined his mouth, and his words dripped. "What have you done?"

Her heart raced and spots danced before her eyes. To have such a conversation with her father was unthinkable. The insinuation was too much to bear. With a hand to her hip, she pushed her fingers to her father's chest. "What are you asking?"

He firmed his lips and had the good grace to look away.

Pulling her palms together in front of her, she laced

her fingers. Elleah pivoted on her heel and strode through the back entrance to return to her hotel room via the service wing. By the time she reached her door, she held her handkerchief to her nose as the tears ran freely down her cheeks. Even in her absence, she had continued to disappoint her father. Nothing was as she had planned. Had she ever had a plan? She gripped the doorknob and laid her forehead against the wood, unable to move any farther. Taking the final step across the threshold seemed too much.

At that moment, the darkness of a tunnel without a light at the end haunted in her imagination. Where would she go now? Would she go? Was there something—anything, to consider between her and Reginald? How would he react now that he knew she was a Mellon and not a Jaundoo?

"My God…" she whispered and banged her head softly against the door. What was she running from, really? Her father? Her past? Her future?

She bit the inside of her lip to take control of her emotions and ran a hand across her cheeks, swiping the tears away. "You're too old to run."

A light hand brushed her hair back from her neck and kissed her softly. "Stop running, then."

Chapter Twelve

Reginald reached around her shoulder and turned her to face him. He framed her face with his hands only swept empty air. His eyes flew open, yet the image of Elleah's hair fanning across his chest was so vivid he could smell her scent. The open space above his bed filled his vision. He noted a yellowish watermark stain on the ceiling and briefly wondered at the cause. Turning to the side, he fanned his fingers across the adjacent pillow. He hadn't imagined it; the indent where her head lay not long ago was still visible.

Could things be different? Had he changed his course? His future?

He didn't need to call her name to confirm she had gone. She filled a room with her presence and she wasn't there. Likely, she had slipped back to her own suite before sun up. He hadn't heard her go. Reginald couldn't remember when he had slept so soundly without the aid of alcohol.

With a lightness he hadn't felt in a long time, if ever, Reginald rolled from the bed and sprang to the floor. He scrunched his bare toes on the carpet. The velvety texture massaged the soles of his feet. He slapped his palms to his thighs. Today, he would find Elleah. They would plan. *What?* He didn't know and laughed out loud, and made his way to the bathroom. Possibilities swirled with the soapsuds of his shower.

After, he puffed his cheeks to shave, holding back his grin. Today was a beautiful day because for once he didn't need to know everything. What did it matter if he didn't have it all figured out? Together, they would come up with something.

He strode across the floor wearing only his towel and reached to brush the curtains aside and check the weather—another sunny day with a light sea breeze. This California weather could create a habit. Unclouded days spent with a partner who made him happy.

Loosening the towel, he pulled it free and dried his hair. Nobody here worried about the weather like they did back east. On the east coast, scrutinizing the weather was a pastime—filler when conversation lagged. Here, whenever he asked about the temperature, people typically looked like he had sprouted another appendage.

Reginald turned toward the bed and felt his loins tighten with memories—soft skin, beautiful eyes, sensual lips, and breathless surrender. He hadn't imagined the act could be so tender, so full, and so complete.

He hadn't heard her leave. He understood her need for privacy. The hotel management would frown upon their dalliance. *She won't have to work here any more.* A contented bubble surged within his chest as he pictured Elleah as his wife.

Returning to the bathroom, he tossed the towel in the corner and grabbed his boxers. In his excitement to be on his way, Reginald missed the leg hole once and chuckled. He leaned forward to the mirror to comb his wayward hair into place and noted the goofy grin. "You're acting like it's your first time with a woman."

Then again, perhaps making love with Elleah was his first time. Love. He lowered his brow and regarded his reflection. There could be no denying he had never before felt this way the morning after. He certainly wanted to feel this way again. Even more than he imagined, the sensation was new and invigorating.

What would they do today? Go for a sail? He paused in mid-motion of zipping his fly. He'd certainly welcome the opportunity to make love on a boat. Reginald chuckled, finished dressing, grabbed his wallet, and opened the door. The door clicked softly behind him and he looked each way, up and down the hall before striding across to her door. Rapping softly, he laid a palm against the wood and leaned closer to listen for any movement inside.

Nothing, not even a shuffle. He rolled back on his heels, one hand in his pocket, and knocked again. He wrapped a hand around the doorknob and then paused. She could be sleeping.

Reginald turned from the door and was surprised to see the maître d' from the restaurant strolling down the hallway.

As he came closer, Reginald noted that the young man wasn't smiling today. "She's gone, sir," he said, in a voice filled with remorse. His hands swung like pendulums in front of his trouser pockets. "Miss Jaundoo left at first light this morning."

Reginald stepped back and looked to her door. "No. You must be mistaken," he replied, his blood running cold. "Perhaps she had meant to leave, but…"

Seeing the shake of the servant's head, Reginald's words trailed.

"I saw to her bags myself, sir." He nodded toward

the closed door. "Her father had been waiting for her. They met her brother in the lobby and left with the dawn."

"Mellon." The word scraped across his throat like a razor blade, leaving a painful wound in its wake.

"Yes. Mr. Mellon insisted they be on their way at once. Poor Miss Jaundoo, excuse me, Miss Mellon." He flapped his hands in front of his chest, then stuffed them in his pockets. "I have come now to understand Mellon is her actual name. She hadn't even changed out of her evening wear."

Reginald suspected his knees might buckle and braced a hand against the wall for support. The texture of the wallpaper scraped against his fingertips. While he slept, his love had been swept away.

"Are you okay, sir?" The maître d' stretched out his arm. His motion stopped a hair's breadth away from actually touching Reginald. "Do you need some air? Water, perhaps?"

"I need more than that." Reginald stepped across the hall and back through his own door.

****

Her chin rested close to her chest. Shamed, Elleah sat beside her father en route to the airport. Her mind wouldn't settle, and her knee bounced reflexively. She tried to focus on one item at a time, but instead, she leapt from thoughts of Reginald, to her father, to what she would do next, to the present situation. A plan of action eluded her due to her inability to concentrate.

When she tiptoed from Reginald's room in the predawn light, she had made up her mind not to pursue a relationship. Their encounter would have to be a sweet dream, a chance meeting. Yes, she had allowed herself to be swept away by his charm, but knowing what she knew, she couldn't allow herself to pursue the situation further. Her feelings would simply have to catch up with the common sense of her mind.

However, any decisions she may have made on her own were all moot now. Before she even had an opportunity to decide what to do next, as she opened her door, her father sprang from her dressing table chair, turned her back toward the hall, and had ushered her through the corridors to the main lobby and into a waiting limo. He obviously bribed the front desk for a key. She had been too stunned by the events to ask.

Elleah lifted the folds of her gown and let them drop with a soft whoosh of air. Without turning to face her father, she addressed him. "I'll not take another step until I change," she said. Resting her palms along her thighs, she determined she would not disgrace herself further by allowing him to see how much his actions impacted her. She wiped a finger under her eye. "I'll never forgive you for this."

She could feel him turn to face her.

"Forgiveness?" He chuckled condescendingly.

"Father, please." Arthur cut in. "You don't need to do this."

Her brother's voice sounded as haggard as he looked.

Her father pointed a finger at Arthur, and hissed, "Stay out of this."

Elleah wished she could steady her racing heart. She felt the seat shift, though she did not alter her focus.

"At the moment, forgiveness has nothing to do with this degradation. That you would give yourself to such a man—"

A blur of movement caused her to turn her head in time to see Arthur grab their father's arm. His green eyes flashed and lips cut a deep slash in his hardened face.

"I said, enough." The words were biting and harsh. "You go too far."

The car bumped throwing them off balance and breaking the strain. The vehicle drew to the curb, followed by the exit of the driver and subsequent banging of the closing door puncturing the heavy silence.

Elleah alighted from the interior, lifted her dress from the grime of the road, and waited for the driver to open the trunk. Before anyone could object, she retrieved her travel case and strode through the glass panels into the airport in search of the ladies' room.

Closing herself within the stall, she hung her head and wondered if her father was correct. Had she disgraced herself? Despite her intention to leave Reginald behind, she couldn't summon any regret for her actions. Yes, she had acted impulsively, allowing her emotions to rule. But the experience had been so sweet. She couldn't regret such a beautiful union.

She scrubbed her palms across her face, pushing the tears back. She hadn't cried yet, however tempted, and she wouldn't start now. She drew a restorative breath, intent to not allow her father's old-fashioned notions to create a feeling of dishonor. The year was 1950, and the world had changed substantially since he and her mother married before the Depression. In actual fact, her mother had been younger than she when Arthur was born.

Elleah ruffled through the bag and changed into a midnight-blue travel pantsuit, with white piping. As the fabric glided across her breasts, she was reminded of Reginald's tender caress and her body grew electric with the memory, feeling every breath of current in the air.

She rushed to the sink and splashed water on her face. Rooting through her purse, she retrieved her compact and made repairs, concealing the red blotches where, despite her best effort, the tears had slipped out. Brush in hand, she wrestled her hair into a tight chignon and secured it with a butterfly pin.

The scent of a heavy floral perfume announced a new arrival to the ladies room before her clipped heels echoed off the tiled walls. With a confident air, a woman not much older than Elleah strode up to the vanity and smiled. She hummed as she touched the lipstick to her mouth.

Elleah glanced across the rows of sinks and nodded. She trained her sights back to her own mirror and wondered if she looked different, now that she felt so different on the inside?

Did she go with Reginald to his room for love? No. Her pulse intensified. Certainly not for him, at any rate. In her opinion, Reginald was too much of a player. Even in the pillow talk after their lovemaking, he spoke of them taking control of the banks and creating a dynasty.

"What a wonderful turn of events that you are who you are." He had smiled down upon her and kissed her forehead, holding her closer. "Together, we can accomplish so much."

Elleah regarded her reflection, dabbed her eyes and

started again. How could she love such a man? So she accepted his kiss and understood right then whatever arched between her and Reginald would not be allowed to blossom. That decision, the knowledge of having only one night with him made her bold. For once, she would take all she could and give with all she had. She explored his body with vigor, marveling in the wonder of the freedom to span her palms across his shoulders, down his tight torso to his narrow hips, and the promise of splendor. His legs scissored between hers and rolled her over, his tongue flicking her nipples, teasing, and drawing them firm. His expert manipulation of her body drew her taut, causing her to arch her back and ache for his touch, reaching for climax.

The memory of the sweet release: the warmth gushing, the tightening, and fusion of her body with his, had Elleah gripping the counter to steady her response and regain her balance. A swift flood of heat flushed across her skin. She stared at her reflection and didn't recognize the person in the mirror. This woman looked sophisticated, chic, poised, and ready. Why then did she allow her father to make her feel like such a child?

The image of this reflected woman was so opposite to how she had viewed herself previously, Elleah averted her gaze to the compact sitting beside her open purse and blinked a couple of times before returning her focus to her own features. The same woman scowled back, her brow puzzled, then cleared. Her eyes sparkled and she winked. Had it been so long since she had really seen herself as others did? A spontaneous giggle erupted and she reached to cover her mouth with her hands.

The humming stopped. "Are you okay?" the lady

in the kitten heels asked as she turned from the sink. "You look a little peaked. The heat here can do that to a person."

Elleah coughed and dampened her fingers. She patted the sides of her neck and under her chin, wiping the excess droplets with a towel. "That must be it." She smiled at the woman, then looked down at her feet. "Your shoes are lovely. Did you get them here? There are some lovely boutiques."

The woman flapped her hand and followed Elleah's gaze. "I'll have to get their names," she said returning her attention to Elleah. "But no. These are from Madison Avenue."

"New York." Elleah nodded. All roads seemed to lead back to the metropolis. "I'm going there today. The next flight out, actually."

"Excellent," the woman said and picked up her purse. "We best hurry, they'll start boarding soon."

Elleah sat in the window seat next to Arthur, second from the front in first class. Her father claimed the aisle seat in the front row. *The New York Times* folded neatly to his preferred section—business, sat across his lap, but she could tell he wasn't concentrating. He hadn't turned a page in some time. He fanned the paper several times in a noisy shuffle, but didn't move on to the next section. Determined to deny any sympathy for his wellbeing, Elleah trained her attention to the tarmac.

The sun had risen and its warmth radiated off the asphalt. Heat shimmers were visible in the still air. People stood at the observation windows of the terminal, waving their goodbyes, and Elleah stretched her fingers across the triple-paned glass in farewell to people she would never know.

The plane lurched forward, and Elleah leaned her brow against the side of the window.

A man caught her attention. Dressed in casual slacks and suit jacket, his tie flapped over his shoulder as he ran from the terminal. He was chasing after their flight. His wavy black hair flopped back from his face and he waved his hand.

"Reginald," she gasped and reached her other hand to brace against the side of the glass.

"What?" her brother asked.

She threw a quick glance at her father's brooding form before answering, her body tight with anxiety. She stared her brother in the eye before training her gaze back through the window to the man she loved. "It's Reginald."

Arthur leaned close to the window to see Reginald's shrinking form in the distance. "You must let him go, Elleah." He drew her hand into his and rubbed a thumb across her knuckles. "A Mellon with a Cavanaugh just would never work."

But hadn't the same sentiment been said about her father and mother?

Chapter Thirteen

Elleah slipped off her gloves and laid them gently on the side table, nodding at the butler who had let her in to the penthouse apartment. She had been back in New York a month and life seemed to have taken on an excessive layer of monotony. Some letters sat in the tray, unopened. Her father had announced her return to the *right* people to have her name circulated socially. She fanned through the correspondence—many addressed to her—invitations to one event or another, and set the bundled stack down, uninterested.

She walked to her room, passing the spacious living room. This had been their family home for as long as she could remember. She paused but a moment, as she always did since she was a child, to admire the spectacular view of the city's skyline. Always building and growing, and yet, from this vantage point, with no unobscured view of Central Park, always the same.

Passing the powder room without much notice, hers was the next door on the left. The canopied bed in any other bedroom would have been the focal point, but Elleah's room was the size of many people's main living area. The large open space was separated into unique quadrants by the placement of furnishings. She had a space for sitting, the bed, of course, for sleeping, and a dressing table. The large walk-in closet off to the right of her entry door featured an array of fashionable clothes, matching every occasion—from riding and tennis to eveningwear. Since her arrival home, her father had spared no expense to win her over with the latest trends from Dior, Cristóbal Balenciaga, Pierre Balmain, Jaques Fath, and Coco Chanel.

Her luggage, mostly unpacked, sat just inside the door.

A prism of color spread across the cream-painted walls from the stained-glass topper on the three gabled windows. She sighed and sat on the ottoman, crossing her ankles and smoothing the lavender silk skirt. Leaning forward, she tucked her chin on her palm as it rested on her knee. Here, in this room, she could imagine her mother's touch again. Closing her eyes, she could smell the citrus scent of her hair. The gentle caress of a caring hand as it brushed the locks back into the latest trends. The soft kiss on the top of her head before her mother left to attend one function or another. The wise words of advice; Elleah smiled and shook her head, guidance those last years of her mother's life, she should have taken note of.

Nothing could change the past, but what she wouldn't give for another one of their *talks*. Elleah repositioned her chin. Sensible conversation was exactly what she needed now. Time to think and contemplate. But the image of Reginald chasing after the plane haunted her. What did his coming after her mean? Was she the lost paycheck, the loss of a business opportunity, or something more?

Surely if his pursuit had meant something more than business, wouldn't he have made contact by now? She had been back in New York for a number of weeks and had seen no sign of him. He would know how to find her now that he knew her name. She had overheard her father grumbling about Declan Cavanaugh to her brother when she passed his study shortly after their return from California. But nothing about Reginald, and certainly neither had broached the subject with her.

She and her father were cordial, but a long way from the loving relationship they once shared. Mostly, her brother acted as intermediary during their meals and evenings out. Evasion offered the best descriptor of her presence in the household. Avoidance of any conversation that would remind them of California. Dodging all notion of the circumstances under which her father had found her. Forestalling any dealing with the situation at all.

The walls of silence had grown more substantial than the brick of the building's framework. Oppressive and caustic, Elleah felt buried under the strain of every smile. Her jaws ached and her temples throbbed. She leaned her head forward to splay her fingers across her brow and lightly massage the throbbing.

Shuffling through the corridor caught her attention. Dropping her hands to fold in her lap, she listened. Just the staff going about their duties. She sat straight and glanced at the practice piano in the corner of her bedroom. Before leaving—no, it had been longer than that—before her mother's death, Elleah had spent most of her spare time seated at the piano, playing and creating vocals. A daily joy. While away, singing had offered solace and comfort. Since her return, however, she had little urge to either play or sing. What was there to sing about, anymore? The very thought of any melody she may consider reminded her of Reginald.

Elleah sighed and rubbed her palms together.

Surely Reginald had returned to New York, for she had seen Catherine at the opera the week before. To Elleah's dismay, Arthur was indeed interested in the cold fish of a woman. Though she did have to admit, Catherine showed quite a bit of vibrancy when on Arthur's arm. Truly, they were a picture together. That could be a result of the fact Arthur genuinely wanted to be in Catherine's presence, as opposed to Reginald, who often had the appearance of being burdened the few times Elleah had seen them together.

"What a small and complex world," she mused, gaining her feet and striding across the room to her bed. She removed the wide-brimmed lavender hat—an exact match for her skirt, and set it on the peach coverlet. She kicked off her patent heels, fluffed her hair, and moved to the closet. The unpacked luggage called to her. She bent to wrap her hand around the handle. She hadn't bothered to empty the contents but for a few essentials—too many memories—too much uncertainty.

"Thinking of running away again?"

Elleah stood straight and grabbed the doorframe for support against tumbling backward. The deep baritone of her brother's voice directly over her shoulder startled her.

"My good lord," she squeaked and took a step back to collide with the wall. She covered her heart with her hands, breathing hard. "I thought you were out."

Her brother's face split into an impish grin. "I'm back."

She stepped out of the closet. "Obviously."

Arthur laid a hand on her shoulder, his lips thinned from a smirk and his brows pinched above his nose.

"You're leaving?" His cultured voice held a note of worry.

Elleah sighed and moved back through the bedroom to the small couch. "I don't know, Arthur." She paced to the window and back to where he remained by her dressing table, like a sentry. "I've been attending the functions and events, as expected. I meet with the ladies' committees Mama belonged to, trying hard to fit in, whatever that means, but…"

"But…it's not you." Arthur's hands moved to his pockets. He leaned his shoulder against the wall.

Elleah tried to swallow. Emotion clogged her throat. In just that casual a move, she was so reminded of Reginald's carefree stance. The pain of longing struck her like a physical blow. "No." She turned to the window, blinking back the tears. "You're right. It's not me. Truthfully, a socialite is not who I want to be."

Arthur scratched his chin and loosened his tie. "What do you want?"

He pushed back from the wall and walked to her. "To run away again—"

"Run to what?" Elleah whirled to look out the window. Instead of the skyline, she saw the golden beach and the gentle surf.

"Him?" Arthur stood close enough for her to hear he held his breath, waiting.

"I've no need to run. You can set your mind to rest." She turned to lay a hand against his cheek. "I'm a grown woman. When I choose to go, I will tell you. I won't hide."

He laid a hand on her shoulder and squeezed gently. "So, you are going, then?"

Her answer, unspoken, lay in a quick nod. Until

that moment, she hadn't realized she had made up her mind.

"Where?" he asked, and then drew her into an embrace. "I'll miss you."

****

Despite his fall from grace, Reginald hadn't quite broken from the family business, as originally intended, but he had certainly taken a detour. To his surprise, Declan did little to dissuade him from his course. Instead, his father seemed resigned to him going his own way forging a new path.

"Extending this kind of credit to the masses is dangerous business," his father espoused, sitting across the large mahogany desk, back in their home branch office.

"Certainly this practice of what they are calling *credit cards* could be," Reginald agreed, shuffling the papers of his dossier. He reached for his briefcase and pulled out several charts for reference. "But these small amounts of credit lines could also be incredibly profitable if we go about it correctly. Instead of one large loan, we offer affordable small loans but to the larger population. More profit for the bank, less risk of default."

After Elleah slipped through his fingers, Reginald had returned to the Del in shock. Immediately, he packed his bags, intent on taking the next flight back to New York to find her. But then what? Was he prepared to propose marriage? Was it fair to seek her out now that he knew her to be an heiress and have her think he only pursued her for her money, as he had done so blatantly with Catherine?

No, he shook his head. He wanted more—needed

more, now that he knew what life could be like, but would she trust his motives? He wanted Elleah, yearned for her. But more important, he wanted Elleah to want him.

While his father shuffled through the stack of charts from his research, Reginald walked to the bar in the corner of the enormous office in the ground floor of their home branch. His fingers grazed the crystal of the decanter but didn't stop. Instead he poured seltzer into a glass and sipped.

In a daze, he had returned to the one city which ever held any appeal to him, only to find the sparkle had come off the gem. Through his mother, he learned of the ripening romance between Catherine and Elleah's brother, Arthur. Somehow, Reginald thought his mother was disappointed in the telling, not from the loss of a daughter-in-law, but from the lack of his own reaction to the news. In that moment, Reginald felt most sorry for his mother and the life she had accepted with his father. To the very marrow of his bones, he knew Elleah would never have acquiesced to such a situation. Equally, he knew he would never want her to.

Inspiration found him in reading the financial section of *The New York Times*. There, he alighted upon an article about Western Union extending credit in the form of charge cards to the blossoming oil companies off the Gulf Coast. How portable money meant for better business and easier access to the corporations' funds. This, in turn, streamlined the negotiation process and enhanced the speed to which they could start drilling.

Reginald laid his glass on the edge of the large desk. "If it could work for the oil industry, surely we could extend the same logic to other business ventures," he explained to Declan. "Think about store credit. This would be portable credit to *any* store, not just a selective few."

As he drew up his plans, Reginald was captivated with the potential. The system of assigning a numbering scheme, which both identified the user of the card and linked back to their bank account, was, in his opinion, brilliantly simple.

"I don't think I'd want to launch something like that here. If these *credit cards*"—Declan fumbled over the words—"went wrong, the public's opinion of our good name could be detrimental to our credibility." Declan sat forward in his chair and steepled his fingers under his chin.

"These cards are already working in select industries, but they're not portable between locations," Reginald shot back. He was prepared for his father's negative reaction and had made alternate plans to pursue the venture without the family's backing.

Declan laid his palms flat on the blotter, "I'm not saying no. I think you're on to something here. We just have to be concerned with reputation as well as availability."

Reginald recognized the spark in his father's eye and left the meeting poised with purpose. Seeking backers elsewhere was an option he preferred to leave on the back burner. Due the success of the meeting with his father, he didn't think he'd have to pursue that avenue. The Cavanaugh empire may have their "California", after all, and not have to worry about marrying the money to do so.

Elleah.

That evening, Reginald found himself trolling the various lounges and bars, hoping for a glimpse of the woman he couldn't forget. Even the sound of her voice would steady his uncertain heart. Taking the stairs to an underground bar, he was doubtful someone of her caliber would be there, but he had to go at any rate, on the off chance she may be singing. Each evening for the last couple of weeks he tried different areas of the city. And as before, hours later, he would stagger home—not from booze—but from disappointment.

What had he been thinking? For her to entertain under the guise of an assumed name was one thing. There was safety for her, on the other side of the country, away from anyone would ever know her. The situation would be clearly difficult for her to pick up a microphone in her own backyard.

Heartsick, he returned to his empty flat. Out of habit, he reached for the decanter of Scotch and switched on the radio to catch the highlights of the baseball game. The Yankees dominated, even after Philly winning the National League Pennant. Pouring himself a glass, he scrutinized the array of color filtered through the amber liquid. In the depths of the liquor, he could almost hear the warm musical notes of Elleah's voice through the reds and rusts.

He set the jug down again and switched the radio over to a music station. Tossing his coat and tie across the chair, he rolled up his shirtsleeves, flung himself into the welcoming cushions of the sofa and kicked off his shoes. If he had ever been inclined to smoke, now would be the time to start. Too bad he hadn't a cigarette in the place.

A particular heartfelt song came across the

airways. The singer embodied the moment. Pain and loss rang clear in every note. Within the lines of the song, Reginald saw Elleah's slim body swaying in time to the rhythm. Closing his eyes, he watched her grasp the microphone as though it were a life preserver. In his memory, he could smell the soft sea scent in her hair.

Reginald sat up and scrubbed the cuffs of his hands across his eyes. Fooling others was easy, fooling himself was not an option. He had to see her again. He had to find her.

Jaundoo.

Chapter Fourteen

Bright Caribbean sun radiated off the white-hot sand. Waves lapped at the shore, hopping over rocks to achieve their goal of crashing on land. Elleah had taken her shoes off and left them up the embankment, close to the tree line. Jumping between the rocks, she stared out to sea. The next island offered only a shimmer of a shadow in the distance. If only her worries could be swept away with the tide.

In the tradition of the islands, a bell sounded in the distance, announcing dinner. She glanced over her shoulder at the big house. On this island, the name Jaundoo was a staple of the economy. Her grandfather owned the very successful sugar plantation his grandfather once worked as a slave. The significance of the passage of time never hit her so hard as here. Elleah bowed her head, she had stayed away too long.

With one last glance over the horizon, Elleah turned back toward the big house. Small cottages dotted the treed beach. Ol' Jaunny, as her grandfather was called, was a good landowner. He took care of his workers, understanding from the very fiber of his being how hard the work on a sugar plantation could be.

As though her thoughts conjured the man, Grand Papere himself trudged across the sand in her direction.

"Come to escort me, yourself?" Elleah asked, smiling and holding out her hand for his.

They linked fingers and then Charles Jaundoo tucked her hand in the crook of his arm. "Of course, *petite cherie*. If I don't keep an eye on you myself, I'm scared you'll up and disappear again."

Elleah's step faltered, she released her hold on his arm, and she lowered her chin to her chest. Tears moistened her eyes and she raised her gaze to the kindly man's face. "Oh, *Papere*, you're as bad as Daddy."

Her grandfather stopped and turned to face her. He brushed a thumb under her eye. "No tears. You're back now." He resumed his hold on her arm and began moving forward again. "But do tell me…what's so bad about your father that you could not work it out?"

Elleah trudged forward, her step heavy. The original reason for her leaving now seemed so pointless compared to the complexity of her current situation. Yes, two-years ago, she and her father quarreled— lots—after the death of her mother. A man who had always been a loving father had turned into someone driven, someone determined to marry her off in the same manner a person unloaded unwanted baggage. Bryan—even the memory of the man sent a revolting shiver down her spine. She had left to prove to her father she was an independent woman capable of making her own choices.

She shook her head. Look where those choices had led: Reginald, a man whose only concern was money.

She struggled to find the words to answer the question, gave up, and leaned her head against her grandfather's shoulder.

He patted her hand.

Glancing up into his leathered face, Elleah read the wealth of experience imprinted in every crag and wrinkle, like the lines on the page of a favorite book. "I don't think you'd understand," she said at last.

"Maybe not, but I think, *ma cherie*, neither do you."

She sighed. "You're right, of course. I miss Mama. She always knew what to say. She understood without ever having to be told."

"Mama's are wise that way; however, Josiah was wise beyond her years. That is why her mother and I didn't stand in her way when she decided to marry your father. We trusted her to know her own heart."

Elleah lifted her head from his shoulder "I've always wondered about that," she said. "To have your daughter marry a foreigner, knowing she would move away and become a stranger."

Papere stopped suddenly, and Elleah would have tripped had she not been holding his arm. "Is that what you think? That your mother was a stranger to your father and unhappy in the marriage?"

Elleah felt the flush in her cheeks. Seldom did her grandfather use this tone with her. "A stranger to society New York. A foreigner used to an island existence, to be swept away by a man totally unfamiliar to her way of life and made to live within his circles. She was an outsider, *Papere*."

He released her hand and laid his upon his hips. He leaned forward at the waist. "Did she tell you that?"

Elleah laced her fingers together in front of her and bit her lip. "Well…no."

Papere stood facing her, glaring. "Did she seem unhappy to you?"

Elleah wished she hadn't opened this can of worms. She was unprepared for his response. She worked through the possible ways of salvaging the situation, but knew from years of experience she would never get away with anything less than the truth with either of her grandparents. Lifting her folded fingers to her chin, she rubbed the knuckles over her skin and pondered his question. What *had* made her think her mother was unhappy? Mama always had time for family—made herself available for her charity work. True she never complained, nor had she ever talked about living anywhere else.

"Do you think we never travelled, my dear girl. Do you think we kept Josiah locked away here?"

"No, but…"

He swept a hand wide to encompass the vastness of his holdings. "Do you think we do not entertain and partake in society?"

"Of course…" Elleah unlaced her hands and dropped her arms to her side, palms facing up. "But surely, *Papere*, having left her home to live in New York with strangers—"

"Where she threw dinner parties for your father's business friends, involved herself in ladies' committees, hosted the mayor, and wrote us endless letters on one event or another," he said with a shake of his head. "Not so very different from what your grandmother has done with me for decades now… No, we never worried for Josiah. Your father made her very happy. She lived the life she was meant to live."

She turned to gaze out over the vast ocean. Where had her assumptions come from? "But, when she died—"

He laid a palm on her shoulder. His grip was tender. "So suddenly and unexpected. So young, with

146

so much still to give…"

Elleah turned in his arms. A tear traced down his cheek reflecting a golden trail. She lifted her pinkie to swipe it away.

He smiled and took her within his embrace to hold her close. "Her death left your father devastated—lost."

Elleah's throat thickened with the reminder of those dark days. Her forehead tucked in the hollow of his shoulder. Then she lifted her head and stepped back as though the veil of fog had been lifted. With clarity, she viewed the months before and after her mother's death with a new perspective. Ashamed of her behavior—the childish running away, the tantrum of reaction to get her own way, her lack of essential communication with the people who loved her most—she hung her head and wrapped her arms around her chest.

Then his strong arms enveloped her again within a warm embrace. The affection contained in the hug reached like a lightning rod through to her heart, where it mattered most. Sniffling her nose, she encircled his strong chest in a returned embrace and felt his strength seep into her.

A cough rattled up his throat from his lungs, and he ended the cuddle to turn back toward the plantation, tucking her hand in his arm. "Come now, Nanny will worry. The sun will soon be down." He handed her a handkerchief, then pointed over his shoulder with his thumb to the ocean and the pink strip of the horizon. "And I have lived my whole life ensuring she is never worried."

Elleah used the embroidered cloth to wiped her face and blow her nose. "Oh, *Papere*, I don't believe that for a moment."

He laughed the echoed barrel laugh that always made him sound as though he was seven feet tall. A clear disguise on his five-foot-ten-inch frame.

Dinner at the big house was both lavish and homey. Surrounded by cousins, family, and their many friends, Elleah was bombarded with local stories of events and activities and a steady stream of questions on her life. What did she do for fun? Why wasn't she married yet? Fashion and more. Becoming used to the ribbing, her head had finally stopped spinning after a couple of days of settling in. She recovered her knack of picking up one topic at a time and then catching another when she could, much like a bear snagging a salmon swimming upstream.

Relaxing after the dinner with a fresh cup of coffee, a couple of young second cousins regaled the family with their theatrics. Grand Papere and Nanny encouraged them with encores, cheering loudly.

Nanny turned and pointed to Elleah. "Sing for us, *Choonkoloonks*." She clapped her hands.

With that announcement, all attention turned to Elleah.

The island term of endearment, meaning sweetheart, brought a glow to Elleah's cheeks. A warm flush crept up her neck. "I don't know—"

Her protests were cut off by her family's boisterous encouragement.

****

The boat docked late afternoon in the shallow bay just as the sun began to settle for the evening. With the back of his hand, Reginald wiped the sweat from his brow. The day had been long, filled with waiting in lines and delays. From New York to Florida, then he'd boarded a smaller plane bound for one of the bigger islands and then chartered a boat for the final leg of the journey. He tossed his jacket over his shoulder and stepped off the gangplank. Exhausted, but buzzing with anticipation, he strolled along the main street off the pier and then checked into what could be termed a 'quaint' hotel.

He paced the small quarters, roaming from the window to the bath and back. He flopped on the bed, recalling Maribel's wise words to him when he had handed over his apartment to her. At long last he had done the right thing and released his sister from the institution their father had placed her after the discovery of her affair with a married man.

Maribel stroked his hand, moisture shimming in her eyes. "You only have this one life, brother." She smiled, released her grip and pulled her shawl about her thin shoulders. "You have made me very happy"—she paused to swipe a tissue across her nose—"but I want you to understand, I have known love and wouldn't have changed a moment."

Reginald stared up at the scarred ceiling of the tropical hotel. The rings around the yellow water marks like counting the age of a tree. The place had stood the test of time.

At one time he would have found his sister's words incredulous. To think she had been sent away for over a year, for a liaison he would have taken for granted as his right as a man, had he gone through with the nuptials to Catherine. Now, he understood.

His gaze moved to the fan in the center of the ceiling. The motor hummed and it looked wearier than he felt as it jolted the air through its paddles. He closed his eyes, only to bounce back up. How could he sleep when he was so close? Doubts held at bay by the simple act of travelling and achieving his destination surfaced to tie his stomach in knots. Was he playing the fool? Would she turn him away? Walking into the bathroom, he splashed water on his face. He gazed at his reflection and couldn't contain the nervous grin. He wouldn't be here if he thought so.

He paced the six steps to stand at the window. The room lacked air. Claustrophobia weighed upon him, and he grabbed his jacket, tossed it over his arm, and fled into the hall. Gulping large gasps of air, he leaned a shoulder against the wall. Gathering his wits, he reminded himself why he was there—one way or another, he would have the answers he needed. She either loved him as he loved her, or she didn't.

Love.

Had he ever expected he would go to such lengths for love?

Huh.

He was as familiar with the great romantic stories as much as the next person and scoffed at their sentimentality his entire life. No, he had always stressed, he would always have a cool head and would never put his pride at such risk.

Reginald paused on the threshold leading onto the street. "Well, look at me now."

He wouldn't allow himself to dwell on the negative. His gut feeling hadn't let him down in the past; surely, it wouldn't desert him now.

Was it just the night before last that he had set his ego aside and approached Elleah's brother, Arthur, to plead his case? To the man's credit, Arthur listened and, with less pondering than anticipated, he told Reginald where to find her.

With little left to chat about, Arthur retrieved his hat from the side chair and tossed his overcoat across his arm. Arthur turned to him. "I'm glad we met face-to-face. My sister means the world to me and I don't want her hurt. But Elleah has always had good intuition about people. Like her, I don't believe the stories about you."

Arthur was about the same age as Reginald, but at the moment seemed significantly older and wiser. He nodded his head. Arthur's narrowed gaze seemed to take his measure from head-to-toe.

"If I gave credence to all I have heard, I would never reveal my sister's location. But, I know she has feelings for you and I can see you do, as well. I don't think it's fair to be separated because of other people's misunderstandings or prejudices."

Reginald could only nod, the snakes in his stomach finally losing their grip.

Not only had Arthur revealed where Elleah was, but he'd given him instruction on how to get there, where to stay, and more importantly, how best to approach Ol' Jaunny.

The clink of ice cubes against the side of a glass brought Reginald back to the present. "Ol' Jaunny, um," Reginald stumbled over the foreign pronunciation. "Be nice to see the place."

"Yes, yes, Ol' Jaunny." The man behind the bar smiled broadly, his teeth glowing bright in the dusky setting. "My mama work for Ol' Jaunny 'til her death."

"Oh, yeah?" Reginald lifted his drink to wet his

lips. He'd hardly touch a drop lately, having lost the need to escape into a bottle. "What was that like for her?" Though he couldn't regret the asking, he was pleased to have any and all information that would help him, but he hadn't expected the parade of stories of Mr. and Mrs. Jaundoo and how much they contributed to the town, the people, or the island.

Taking a moment to assess the ceiling and the surrounding décor, Reginald eyed the barman and came to a decision. "Can I see the place?"

With a vigorous nod of his head, the man replied, "For sure, I take you."

Reginald straightened on his stool "Now?"

The barman reached behind to untie and remove his apron. He retrieved his keys from under the counter and shook them in the air. "Yes, now," the man replied.

Reginald stood. "Who will watch your bar?" He was mystified at how the man was so willing to up and leave his place of business to take him to the plantation.

He shrugged his shoulders. "I close, then I come back and open again." And with that, the man shooed the few patrons out with promises of stories upon his return.

Reginald chuckled, thinking the man must consider the event some grand adventure. He placed his hat on his head and smiled. This certainly was a journey. Life with Elleah could be the grandest of adventures.

After a harrowing half hour drive along the cliff road, they reached the entrance to the plantation. Even at night, Reginald could see the place was vast. The trees lining the lane formed a darkened canopy in the purplish light of early evening. Ahead, tiki torches provided the elegant lighting at the end of the tunnel.

Sweat trickled down Reginald's spine, and his breathing grew rapid with the symbolism. Elleah was his light, and his journey through the darkness was finally at an end.

The bartender tapped the steering wheel, then pointed through the cracked windshield. "Much more beautiful during the day," the driver said. "You come back tomorrow. I take you."

"Yes," Reginald agreed, his heart taking on a new tempo. "Tomorrow."

The man started to turn the car around.

On impulse, Reginald opened the door.

The driver grabbed his sleeve. "What you doin'?" He slammed on the brakes. "You get yourself killed."

Reginald tore his gaze away from the plantation. "Sorry." He held up his palm in peace. "So sorry. I'll walk back."

The driver patted his arm and grinned. "You crazy? It's as dark as pitch. You'll get lost, fall off the side of the island, and drown in the ocean. Nobody see you again, and I'll have no good stories to tell."

Reginald chuckled at the dramatic images. "I promise I won't fall into the ocean, and I'll make sure you have plenty of stories to tell." He slipped the man a few bills and got out of the car.

The driver waited for Reginald to exit and then slipped the car into gear, waving in exuberance as he drove off into the night.

The fresh air smelled sweet of sugar and citrus with a hint of salt off the ocean. He paused by the gated entrance and waited for his heart to resume a regular rhythm. Stepping to the edge of the lane, he glanced over his shoulder and watched the taillights of the car fade into the distance. The gate stood open, welcoming, and sure of his decision, began to trek along the long drive. Beyond the torches, the glow from the house was just visible in the distance.

When the notes from a husky voice reached him, Reginald froze in his tracks, his heart slamming against his ribcage. She was here, and she was singing. He hadn't expected to hear her voice. He was transported back to the California beach where her throaty tones first entranced him. Again, the melody touched him with a tender caress. A part of him knew even then, what he was sure of now. He was a man in love.

"Hey, you."

The snarl was a mere forerunner to the beefy hand that crashed upon his shoulder as he was grabbed from behind, and his arm wrenched up behind his back.

Chapter Fifteen

The first song Elleah sang had been light and breezy. Familiar with the words, her family and their friends joined in.

Pausing for breath, Elleah brushed a hand over her hair to swipe the loose ends back from her cheeks. She stood by the polished black piano and waited for the first strikes of the keys of the next melody to sink in. The longevity of the notes blended to fill the room with additional color of harmony. A slow number. She breathed in and released the air slowly, preparing for the moment.

Her uncle Orlo played with the artistry of a concert pianist. Head bent in concentration, his long fingers splayed across the keys, moving with the rhythm of a lover's caress.

Biding her time, she laid her palm on the mirrored surface. Elleah closed her eyes and let the waves of the piece wash over her. When she opened her eyes, Orlo winked at her. Then he lifted a hand, and with the flick of his wrist gave her the cue to start. Smiling back, she relaxed in sync to his lead.

The sensual song told the story of island lovers separated through no fault of their own. Looking out over the small, intimate gathering, Elleah felt the lyrics take hold. Her mother had sung this very same ballad many times, and through that early memory, Elleah heard her mother's voice, not her own.

By the time she completed the first chorus and other family members sang the background chant, Elleah was immersed. As she swayed to the beat, she felt Reginald's arms around her. Within the pauses, Elleah imagined his lips travelled over her neck, across her jaw, until he swept her away with the touch of his lips to hers. Through his touch she had felt complete, protected, cherished, alive, and confident. Then, all at once, *she* was the island lover separated from her one true love—a soul mate who, despite their own individual flaws, were somehow made for each other.

Misunderstanding after misunderstanding had swept her away, end over end, with passing time leaving her to wonder which way was the right way. She had been caught in a current, crashing against an unknown rock and unable to make land. Her wandering began with the loss of her mother. That emptiness in her life hadn't altered until she met Reginald. Despite what her brain may have cautioned against, in her heart, he filled the void. Only here, surrounded by her mother's people, did she feel the acute loss of him—the man—his companionship—his simple presence. Her interaction with Reginald provided her a compass, a way forward—through the storm with the promise of coming out the other side whole.

Yet, she had again walked away.

Could she find her way back?

Elleah realized now, as she scanned the people in the room, in her pain of loss, she had neglected to notice others—most especially her own father—who had felt the very same sorrow, adrift without the anchor of stability her mother had provided. *If Mama were here now*, Elleah thought, she would ask her opinion on Reginald. Could he be trusted? Would her love be returned? Was he worth the risk? Would he love her for who she was, not for where she came from, or the potential of acquiring wealth?

She curled her hand into a fist. Damn, she should have been honest with him. How could she expect someone to be honest with her if she were not willing to provide the same?

A wet trail of tears crept down her cheeks as she finished the final notes of the song. Her heart ached and her mind filled with questions, doubts, and uncertainty. She knew what she wanted, but was she crazy for wanting it?

Could she be strong enough to swim back through the tides of disaster and find her peace?

Silence surrounded her, and she opened her eyes.

Her family stared, muted by the last strains of the melody. Sympathy stretched their features.

Striving for composure, Elleah swiped a finger across her cheek. Heat rose up her neck and the urge to be alone consumed her. "Excuse me." She stumbled a couple of steps, then fled the room. She walked with as much dignity as she could muster. Glancing over her shoulder, she called back in a stiff voice. "I'll be right back."

Elleah raced through the length of the house until she stepped out onto the veranda. Relief budded like a blossom, and she breathed deeply of the fragrant air—fresh-cut grass, neatly trimmed hedges releasing their sap, and a multitude of flowers. The stars dotted light into the pitch-black of the sky, while the surf rumbled in the distance, hidden by the night. She gripped the railing and stood and stared, realizing how small and insignificant her worries may seem in this big wide world, yet they still managed to consume her.

The lights from vast rooms flooded the manicured grounds, illuminating the near gardens, which ringed the house, following the lines of the wraparound terrace. Elleah pounded the banister until pain shot up her nerve endings. She hung her head. Hot tears splashed onto the backs of her hands, and she didn't try to stop their barrage.

A fragrant musk announced the presence of her grandmother a half-second before the slender arm wrapped around Elleah's shoulders.

Nanny squeezed her close. "What troubles you, *Choonkoloonks?*" she asked, running a hand over Elleah's hair. "Relieve your soul and tell your ol' Nanny."

"Oh, Nanny, if only I could. If I understood myself—my decisions—my actions. I have been so naïve and ignorant." She sniffled and pulled her embroidered handkerchief from her sleeve to dab her face.

"Naïve, maybe, my *Choonkoloonks*, but never ignorant, eh? Look in your heart. Perhaps the island air will add the substance you need to figure out a solution," her grandmother crooned.

Her soft voice filled the air with aged wisdom, so reminding Elleah of her mother's way. She leaned into Nanny's embrace.

"An argument with yourself on the inside sounds significantly different when you talk it out with someone who loves you."

Nanny's wise words and earnest face lent

confidence. Elleah tucked her head against her grandmother's shoulder. Swallowing the thickness in her throat, she coughed lightly and then the words rumbled forth in an avalanche of emotion. "I'm ashamed. So ashamed, Nanny. I ran away without even trying to understand. I disgraced Mama's memory by my unwillingness to try, and now I don't know what to do. I don't know who I am, who I'm supposed to be. I met a man I'm not supposed to love, who can't love me back—not for the *real* me."

Her grandmother squeezed her tighter. Elleah lifted her head to see Nanny lift her half-moon brows in question.

"He can't know me, Nanny. How can he? I didn't let him. For heaven's sake, I don't know me anymore. Not when I have been so cowardly."

"No, no, my dear, stop confusing your actions. You could never be cowardly. Confused—perhaps. We all go there from time-to-time. But I cannot believe what has been done cannot be mended. I did not live all these great long years without seeing such things." Her grandmother traced a hand over Elleah's hair and tucked a lock behind her ear. "If you believe you are worthy of his love, you will be loved. You love this man?"

Elleah pulled back and laid her palms against her heated cheek, fingers to her temples, hoping to clear the mist. She stopped to consider Nanny's words and nodded. "But will he love me? And if he does, how can I ever be worthy when I've been so selfish?"

Nanny shook her head and took hold of Elleah's shoulders, her strong fingers squeezing through the thin fabric of her dress. "Stop this right now. We all must journey at some point in our lives. This is your journey."

Visions of her father's hurt, her treatment of Arthur, Reginald running across the tarmac and her always leaving, resisting, flooded her with sorrow. How could she make amends? She needed to be accountable. "No, Nanny. You see, I keep running away, thinking my problems will be left behind." She braced her palms against her eyes and swayed, taking a step back toward the balustrade.

"You cannot change what has been done, nor should you try, child. You can't start over…but you can start from here."

Elleah lifted her head, interested, and hiccupped. "From here?"

"Yes." Her grandmother nodded while she continued to stroke Elleah's hair. "From here. One step, every day."

Elleah sniffled and wiped her nose gently across the handkerchief. "But where will I go, what will I do? I love a man who will never love me for who I am—"

"The hell I won't," a cultured voice growled, his steps heavy and intent as he trod across the length of the veranda.

****

"I *know* who you are. I've travelled half the globe to find you, hoping against hope you would accept *me* for *who* I am, my warts and all." Reginald stopped just outside the ring of light that surrounded the two women.

His heart pounded so loudly in his ears he was afraid he wouldn't be able to hear Elleah speak after his intrusion. He had listened, pained by her sorrow, afraid she wept for someone else. In realizing she spoke of him, it was all he could do not to run and sweep her up in his arms. Losing his momentary burst of courage, he dropped his arms to his sides and waited for some signal, not knowing what that may be.

When the older lady—no mistaking the family resemblance between her and Elleah—stepped toward him with her hand extended, Reginald remembered his manners.

He grasped her hand to sandwich it between his own. He bowed marginally, his eyes downcast to the floorboards, then raised them to meet her gaze, while retaining his hold. "Do excuse my language, madam. I'm Reginald Cavanaugh, and I am in love with your granddaughter."

"You do make quite the entrance, Mr. Cavanaugh," she replied with a broad grin. "I'm Miriam Jaundoo. I don't think Elleah and I have gotten to the specifics of your identity, just yet."

He released her hand and stood tall. "It is my pleasure." He returned her smile. "I'm more than willing to stick around for the specifics myself. I would be interested."

Without casting a glance her way, he heard the in-drawn breath from Elleah. He bit his cheek to prevent a nervous chuckle from escaping. He wanted to spend a lifetime teasing her, getting to know her, baiting her, and most importantly, loving her. If this stately woman standing before him—still holding his gaze, supporting him without words—was any indication to what he had to look forward to in the years to come, he was all in.

Miriam winked and stepped back to Elleah's side. "You are welcome, Mr. Cavanaugh—"

He linked his hands behind his back and remembered to breathe. "Reginald, if you please."

"Yes, Reginald, and it does please me. Well, Elleah?" She turned to her granddaughter. "You were saying?"

Reginald faced Elleah. His gaze searched hers. Sadness stretched the corners of her eyes, yet he detected a spark in their depths and his heart leapt against his ribs. His hands felt the slight tremor of his rapid pulse and his stomach tied itself within a vault of knots—all proof positive if she didn't accept him, his heart would surely cease beating all together. He fidgeted from foot to foot, like a schoolboy, as Elleah stared between him and her grandmother, mouth opening and closing without sound.

Nanny stepped closer to Elleah and pulled her granddaughter close. "Take your first step from here, child." Releasing Elleah, she turned to Reginald. "You are welcome to stay. I will leave you two to your privacy." With those words, she drifted through the doors to disappear within the expansive house.

His left hand squeezed his right behind his back. He focused on Elleah, waiting, sweat starting to trickle down his spine.

Her head tilted to the side and her brows rose. "You came? For me?"

Quiet words he had to strain to hear. He took one tentative step closer. "Yes." Here was his chance. "For you. Not for your money, your name, your father's business, or your family's assets—none of that matters. In California, you showed me life's potential." He paused to draw breath and his arms fell to his sides, palms positioned to the heavens. "You showed me what my life could be like, and I can't go back. You ruined me."

A tear on her cheek sparkled like a diamond as it hovered and thickened with moisture before trailing down her face. He lifted a hand and swept the teardrop onto his fingertip. "You see, I love you, Elleah. And from now on, I want these to be only happy tears."

In the light cast from the open garden doors, through the enormity of her irises, he saw the depths of her soul exposed. In this look, she granted him access. He understood the precious gift she bestowed. A ship finding safe harbour, the knots in his stomach released and his blood ceased its roar through his veins.

Her eyes rounded and a touch of mischief lit her gaze. A small dimple tweaked the corner of her mouth. "And how will you ensure that?"

The palms of his hands framed her face, his fingers laced through her hair, and he pulled her to him. "I have my ways."

She reached her arms up to fold around his neck and laid her forehead against his chest. "You came."

"Where you go, I go."

"And where you go"—she lifted her face to his, brushing her lips along his—"I shall be by your side."

Remembering her conversation with her grandmother, Reginald stroked his thumbs a gentle caress across her cheeks. He lowered his brow to hers, contentment had freed his spirit. "Love will be our journey together."

Elleah leaned forward to touch her forehead to his. "Together."

If you enjoyed this book, you will want to read *FROM THE FRONT DESK,* book two in the Gentle Surf series by Lori Power. Here's a sample:

Chapter One

Sweat dripped from the ends of Wendee's short hair. The sandy blonde strands appeared dark brown with the accumulated moisture where they flopped in rhythm to her step, in front of her eyes. She huffed and reached a hand up to swipe the curtain of bangs back from her brow. The dribble tickled its way along the edge of her ear. She rubbed the moisture from her palm on her shorts without breaking her stride. Her feet slapped along the sidewalk, relishing the freedom of running outside. Even at six in the morning, the California coastal island of Coronado was hot compared to what she was used to in the Midwest, and the sun wasn't even up yet. By the time the sun reached its summit, she'd be surrounded in air-conditioned luxury.

This time of year, at home, was usually all hockey and hot coffee. Her tongue peeked out to run along her lips imagining the caffeine boost.

Not her home any more. Roger had seen to that.

Wendee slowed her speed as she approached the entrance for the special forces Sea, Air and Land—SEAL—training base. One of three on the island. Could there be a safer place in America than the island of Coronado? Someone at the front desk at the Hotel Del Coronado had told her how many military installations there were between here and San Diego, but she forgot.

Suffice to say more than a handful. She hoped that would be enough.

Slowing her tread, she tapped the light pole in front of the guard station, tag fashion. Not waiting to see the officer, Wendee turned and retraced her steps along the residential road now busy, despite the early hour, with military personnel heading to work. The beach flanked her right, shadowed in the early morning, compared to the dark mass of the ocean beyond. Beautiful houses followed the road along her left. The A-frame, Cape-style beach homes left her in little doubt to the enormity of their worth.

She rubbed her chin along the shoulder of her T-shirt to clear the drip and winced. The bruises were slow to heal.

The electronic voice from her running application on her smart phone updated her pace and distance. The halfway mark. She squinted her eyes and increased her pace.

Within the last month of living on the island, she'd found lodging and a job. The pride of her accomplishments lifted her lips. She felt more independent than she ever had. It seemed unlikely Roger would try to look for her, but she didn't want to assume. She had done that more than once and ended up at the ass end of that statement.

Contriving a way to contact her brother, Walter, had been an activity in imagination. He'd be the only who would care enough to wonder where she went. They were each other's only family. Still, she didn't want him involved. He could take care of himself, she wasn't worried about that, but he'd had his own issues over the years and didn't need someone like Roger casting suspicion.

The front desk position offered the perfect solution. Twice now she'd sent him post cards she purchased from gas stations while driving here. No return address. The note was simple, but cryptic, providing enough information to let him know she was okay. Then when Wendee had a few conversations with guests, she would hand them the card with a buck for postage and ask them to mail it from their hometown.

"My brother likes to collect stamps post marked from various locations." Here she would shrug. "I can't travel everywhere, but since you're from…" It really didn't matter where the guest was from, just so long as it was outside the state of California.

With the two she had sent so far, she'd been greeted with smiles and "isn't that a marvelous idea."

She'd yet to receive a response, but then again, Walter wasn't much for correspondence.

Wendee glanced around before crossing the intersection. She loved it here so far. Friendly people with a real sense of community, yet she was able to keep to herself without worrying about causing suspicion. She shrugged her shoulders, wondering at the winding road that was life. Who'd have guessed, a winding bridge, a marvel of engineering skill, would intrigue her enough to cross over to the other side both literally and figuratively.

Diverging from the sidewalk, Wendee bounded down the small flight of wooden stairs to the pathway separating the beach from the resort-style hotel. The place was ageless and as cherished as a prized antique. The iconic red roof had attracted visitors for more than a century, yet she had never heard of it before applying for a position. Thank God for her phone and Google.

Contrary to the main road, on the boardwalk, only a handful of people were out this time of the morning. The fresh sea salt air brought a sense of rejuvenation and hope, a feeling which had become so foreign, she thought she had lost capability. Another watchtower loomed ahead, the second angle in the triad of military bases on the island. She hoped to use some of earnings, once she paid her landlord, to rent a bike for the afternoon and explore further afield. Driving slowly through residential streets in a car would raise more than a few antennae. She glanced at the two guards at their post and snickered at the thought.

The entrance to the military annex, with the twelve-foot walls, contrasted sharply with the beachfront where it met at the end of the boardwalk. However, the message was clear, no civilians past this point. Typically, Wendee would pull another tag and go back to the other side, not yet familiar enough with the island to venture along the other streets and find the third base. But not today.

She had noticed other runners move across the sand and run along the water. So today, feeling more courageous than before, she stepped off the path and made her way across the sand to jog closer to the surf. Unlike the boardwalk, here the sand was hard packed, perfect for running. The joy of lengthening her strides and racing with the wind, watching water play with the shore renewed her energy. The sun cast a merry glow from her left and landmass of Mexico materialized like a purple shadow emerging from the blue-green of the ocean, ahead on her right.

Wendee looked down at the sand that had begun to

shimmer like golden dust in the growing light and noticed a sand dollar. Almost toppling, she stopped and picked up the delicate shell and ran a fingertip over the skeletal embossing. Straightening, she cradled the treasure in her palm and looked out to the horizon. Stretching her gaze across the vista, she watched the last flicker from stars fade from view. The music from her headphones matched the scenery. The artist spoke of new beginnings and for the first time, Wendee believed this could be true.

Following the skyline from the north to south, fishing rigs and patrol boats alike shared the seascape. She stroked the sand dollar nestled in her hand. Yes, this could be home.

A large hand tapped her shoulder and Wendee jumped and turned almost dropping the shell. Her heart thudded. She folded her fingers around the sand dollar and held it to her breast before training her focus on the intrusion.

A sweat-stained vee filled her view. She ran her gaze up, over broad shoulders, across a squared jaw, roughened with bristles to the most stunning silver-gray eyes. Framed by dark lashes and lighter, sun bleached, straight brows, they crinkled at the edge as he peered back.

She quickly observed his reddened face glittered with perspiration. Over his ears, wet, honey-toned curls stuck out from beneath a bandana. His mouth, curved into a smile, moved, yet she heard nothing. Those razor-sharp eyes seemed to sparkle with merriment, softening the effect and his brows rose.

Wendee shrugged her shoulder higher to brush the edge of her shirt over her cheek and wipe away some perspiration. Her stomach clenched in awareness of his close proximity. "What?" Her voice croaked, sticking halfway up her windpipe. She coughed and struggled to hear what he was saying.

His lips, well formed and etched perfectly within the growth of day-old beard, moved but still she could hear nothing. The song playing spoke of a lover's caress and she could easily imagine those lips finding all of the perfect places along her body in dire need of some attention. She shook her head to clear the unwelcomed thought and sweat rained from the movement. Embarrassed, she stole a look at her feet, wanting nothing more but to shuffle away, take a shower and meet him when she looked and smelled significantly better than she did right now.

Seeming mesmerized, she watched his hand, with long tapered fingers move toward her. She rolled her shoulder back from his approach and he smiled, flicked his fingers and her earbud fell out.

"Oh."

His smile activated dimples in his cheeks and her knees tingled with a funny little tickle. Heat rushed up her neck and flooded her cheeks.

"You better get going," he said and pointed with a thumb over his shoulder.

Get going? Why? Was he some sort of trainer? How did he know she wasn't done her run?

Wendee wasn't prepared to be bossed around. As though dosed with cold water, she shrugged and tried to face the sea, but again his gaze captivated her and she stood staring.

"No," he persisted, and lifted his chin a fraction in the same direction as his thumb. "You ought to get going."

Wendee couldn't see past the broad shoulders and he stood at least a foot taller than her, so whatever was over his shoulder was his business. Remembering her pledge for independence and taking a grip on the distraction he was causing, she retrieved the ear bud where it swung loose below her chest and lifted it to her ear. Before corking it in place inside her ear, she tilted her head and smiled. "Thanks Mate. I'll get going in my own good time."

The dimples deepened when he grinned down at her. With an unhurried movement, he pulled the rag from his head and wiped his face. The loose curls drifted like clouds settling. He retied the bandana and gave her the once over with those sharp-colored eyes. He glanced again over his shoulder and shrugged. "Suit yourself then."

With that he turned and his long legs carried him toward the Hotel Del Coronado. The loose gray shorts hung down to his lower thigh, but curved nicely against his rear, revealing sculpted buttocks. It cost her nothing to look.

But then she twisted around fully, curious to what he had been pointing to. What curiosity lay inland? Over the dunes, positioned well back of the breakwater, black-clad SEAL training teams swarmed like ants, leaving the nest. In teams of eight, four each side of a dingy, they were making for the water. Everywhere she looked, drill squads descended. Within minutes she'd be swarmed and completely in their way. Abandoning her poetic ponderings of new beginnings, Wendee secured the earbud in the same motion with her feet kicking up sand. As fast as she could, she followed Mr.

Wellmade's tracks. Not pausing, or losing stride until she again reached the boardwalk. Once there, breathing heavily, Wendee turned back to see the beach simmering with military personnel deep into exercise maneuvers. In the short amount of time she'd been in the island, the one thing she had heard—and heard often—SEALs take their training very seriously.

Glancing back along the boardwalk, there was no sign of man. That was likely a good thing. No one to bear further witness to her embarrassment. Looking down at her garb, she winced. She didn't go in for the fancy running gear. Her gym shorts were splattered with paint stains of better memories. The loose garment hung to her knees and were ripped in several places she didn't care about—until she did—when a well-made man stopped to chat. No, she corrected, to warn her she was in the way. What an impression she must have made. She picked up the edge of her T-shirt plagued with the gray sickness…maybe she'd invest in a better shirt if she knew she would meet up with lightning eyes again.

"Puh," she breathed and dropped the shirt from her fingers. "Whatever."

Casting one last glance around confirming he was nowhere in sight, she resumed her usual pace. Wendee finished her run and walked back to her small basement flat, all the while keeping an eye out for the handsome stranger. What did she care any way?

Despite herself, she did.

A word about the author…

Turning passion into words in print is a dream come true for Lori Power.

From radio host (best job ever!), DJ, news reporter to newspaper journalist, like many authors, Lori has been writing most of her life.

In writing, Lori has discovered a truism: everyone has a great story to tell. All you need to do is listen. Over the years, with all the people Lori has met previously and daily, both professionally and personally, with an ear to the ground, readers can often find these "characters" fictionalized in stories.

Not confined to one genre, Lori has published select children's books and one cookbook, based on a gluten-free diet, as well as non-fiction industry blogs.

Lori's first novel, *Storms of Passion*, was published by The Wild Rose Press under their Champagne line in 2014.

Collaboration is important to improving one's craft, and Lori is an active member of the TransCanada Romance Writers, Romance Writers of America, The Alberta Romance Writers Association, and both a critiquing group and a beta reading weekly group.

Lori looks forward to continuing to find the good story; hashing out a scene, having fun with a character, and writing the story she would love to read.

www.loripowerwriter.com

Thank you for purchasing
this publication of The Wild Rose Press, Inc.

If you enjoyed the story, we would appreciate your
letting others know by leaving a review.

For other wonderful stories,
please visit our on-line bookstore at
www.thewildrosepress.com.

For questions or more information
contact us at
info@thewildrosepress.com.

The Wild Rose Press, Inc.
www.thewildrosepress.com

Stay current with The Wild Rose Press, Inc.

Like us on Facebook

https://www.facebook.com/TheWildRosePress

And Follow us on Twitter
https://twitter.com/WildRosePress

www.ingramcontent.com/pod-product-compliance
Lightning Source LLC
Chambersburg PA
CBHW072123170626
46813CB00004B/1668